Coasting

Gold Hockey #8

Elise Faber

COASTING
BY ELISE FABER
Newsletter sign-up

COASTING
Copyright © 2020 Elise Faber
Print ISBN-13: 978-1-946140-68-5
Ebook ISBN-13: 978-1-946140-67-8
Cover Art by Jena Brignola

GOLD HOCKEY SERIES

Gold Hockey (all stand alone)
Blocked
Backhand
Boarding
Benched
Breakaway
Breakout
Checked
Coasting
Centered
Charging
Caged
Crashed
A Gold Christmas
Cycled
Caught
Cap

Gold Cast of Characters

Heroes and Heroines:

Brit Plantain (Blocked) — first female goalie in the NHL, loves boy bands

Stefan Barie (Blocked) — captain of the Gold

Sara Jetty (Backhand) — artist and figure skater

Mike Stewart (Backhand) —defenseman for the Gold, romance guru

Blane Hart (Boarding) — center for the Gold, number 22

Mandy Shallows (Boarding) — trainer and physical therapist

Max Montgomery (Benched) — defensemen for the Gold, giant nerd

Angelica Shallows (Benched) — engineer at RoboTech, also a giant nerd

Blue Anderson (Breakaway) — top forward in the league and for the Gold

Anna Hayes (Breakaway) — Max's former nanny, no relation to Kevin Hayes

Rebecca Stravokraus (Breakout) — Gold publicist, makes killer brownies, known at PR-Rebecca

Kevin Hayes (Breakout) — forward for the Gold, no relation to Anna Hayes

Rebecca Hallbright (Checked) — nutritionist for the Gold, plethora of delicious vegan recipes, known as Nutrionist-Rebecca

Gabe Carter (Checked) — doctor, head trainer for the Gold

Calle Stevens (Coasting) — assistant coach for the Gold, former national team member

Coop Armstrong (Coasting) — talented forward on the Gold, addicted to historical romance audiobooks

Mia Caldwell (Centered) — 5th degree black belt, brings the snark

Liam Williamson (Centered) — Gold forward finding his love for the game, charming and pushy in equal measures

Charlotte Harris (Charging) — new Gold GM, hates losing and the game Chubby Bunny

Logan Walker (Charging) — defensemen for the Gold, skills include: cockiness and being able to buy presents that make Charlotte squirm

Devon Scott (Block & Tackle) — former player, current owner Prestige Media group

Becca Scott (Block & Tackle) — Devon's assistant

Additional Characters:

Bernard — head coach

Richie — equipment manager

Dan Plantain — Brit's brother

Diane Barie — Stefan's mom

Pierre Barie — Stefan's dad, owner of the Gold

Spence — former goalie, married to Monique, daughter Mirabel

Monique — married to Spence, former model

Mirabel — daughter of Spence and Monique

Mitch — Sara's boss

Allison and Sean — Blane's parents

Pascal — Devon Scott's security lead

Roger Shallows — Mandy's dad

Grant and Megan — Devon's parents

ONE

COOP

"**S**o, in conclusion, you need to get your fucking head out of your fucking ass," Calle snapped into her cell phone. "Otherwise, I swear to fucking God I will never, *ever* talk to you again."

Coop had just exited through the arena door, the entire team having gathered to watch their nutritionist and newfound best-selling author, Rebecca, on a national morning show promoting her book. The shy, quiet redhead was unassuming but also a major reason the Gold were currently the number one team in the league. She'd come up with the diet plan the entire team was following, which was a major source of their increased energy and shortened injury recovery time.

He knew he, for one, had never felt better, thanks to Rebecca and the rest of the training staff.

But another one of the reasons the team was doing so incredibly well was standing right in front of him, forehead pressed to her clenched fists, one of which still clutched her cell phone.

Calle Stevens, newest assistant coach for the Gold and former national team member. She was tall for a woman and slender, but also deceptively powerful, with thighs, shoulders, and arms that bespoke of the graceful and fierce player she'd been on the ice. She might have blown out her knee, but that inner athlete never completely faded. Add in a head for the game that out thought most coaches twice her age, and she had been a huge boon to the team when they'd picked her up.

She was also even.

That was the best description Coop could think for her. Never raised her voice, always ready with a smile or joke. Stern sometimes, yes. Tough, for sure. But she wasn't a yeller.

And after playing hockey from the time he was five, he'd been on plenty of teams with yellers.

Calle sighed and pocketed her phone, staring off into the distance for several long moments before sweeping her long brown hair back into a ponytail and turning to reenter the building.

Which was the moment that he realized he should have moved.

Coop should have gone when he'd stumbled onto the conversation that was obviously private since she'd stepped outside to take it.

But he hadn't because . . . well, Calle wasn't the type of person who screamed into cell phones, who took long, centering breaths before dashing her thumb under each eye, as though she were wiping away tears.

She didn't cry. She didn't yell. She—

Was staring right at him.

"Hey," she said after a long moment, blinking the distance from her gaze, though he noticed she still focused on a point over his left shoulder and not on him. Her cheeks were flushed pink, but under that, her skin was even paler than normal. More porcelain than peaches and cream. "You have a chance to review those tapes from Dani?" she asked.

Dani was their video coach, and the woman was able to cut, prep, and send clips of games to the team's tablets faster than most people could unlock their phones. Calle had asked her to send over a package the previous day, and he'd watched them this morning. He nodded. "Yeah, thanks for that. I think it'll be helpful for me on the breakout. Especially against Tampa Bay."

Calle brushed a hand through her hair. "Good, good," she said distractedly.

He frowned. "Are you okay?"

"Hmm?" She finally met his eyes. "Yeah. I'm great."

Except her tone was completely off.

"Calle," he said.

Anger edged into her expression, mouth opening, and Coop braced for some of the same pissed-off woman that he'd overheard on her call. But almost as quickly, that fury faded, and her pretty brown eyes filled with tears.

"I'm fine," she whispered. "I'll be fine."

"Who was on the phone?" he asked.

"Doesn't matter."

"*Calle.*"

"It doesn't." She shook her head brusquely, sucked in a breath.

Maybe he would have let it go, let *her* go as she walked by, kept things between them strictly professional.

But then he saw the tear.

Glistening in the morning light as it escaped the corner of her eye.

Without thinking, he caught her arm.

"You're not okay."

She shuddered to a stop when he touched her, not fighting the grip, chin dropping to her chest. "No," she said, "you're right. I'm not okay."

"Who was on the phone?" he asked gently.

Her jaw went tight. "My ex."

Fury blazed through him. "Did he hurt you?" he growled.

A shake of her head. "Not like you're thinking." She sucked in a breath. "He broke my heart."

Coop's own heart gave a twinge. "I'm sorry, Calle. That's—"

"Fucking stupid." Another tear joined the first, dripping down the pale skin of her cheek.

"It's not stupid to have loved someone," he said gently.

Her eyes went fierce. "It's incredibly stupid when the person who supposedly loves you right back doesn't give a damn that you're pregnant."

His jaw fell open. He knew it did.

But Calle? Even, gentle *Calle* had gotten knocked up and—

"Yup," she said, brushing by him. "See? Really *fucking* stupid."

And without another word, she disappeared into the rink.

Two

CALLE

"Oh God, oh God, oh God," she whispered, the realization of what she'd just said to Coop sinking in now that she was alone in her office.

Pregnant.

She *thunked* her head down onto her desk. "How could you have been so stupid, Calle Stevens?"

To think that when she'd taken the test that morning, she'd actually had a sliver of hope that she and Jason might get back together, that they might be able to work out their differences, that it might be what jumpstarted their relationship again.

Yeah, *that* never went wrong.

Because having a baby *always* fixed relationships.

"Fuck," she muttered and forced herself to straighten. She couldn't think about this now. There was work to do, and it wasn't like anything was going to change in the next nine months.

Nine. Months.

Oh God.

This was actually happening.

She'd spent her entire life keeping her head down and not making stupid mistakes and . . .

She'd made up for that two months ago.

That was what happened when people got lonely.

They did idiotic things.

Like sleeping with their ex when he'd popped into town while on a road trip. Like dating a hockey player in the first place. Like dating a hockey player who was in the AHL and pissed that he wasn't in the NHL. One who wasn't happy that she'd gotten selected to coach an NHL team.

She'd understood.

It was hard to see someone else get breaks and move up in the world and be left behind.

God, how she got that.

She'd watched from the sidelines as her teammates had scored a gold medal, crutches under her arms, standing and cheering, and so fucking thrilled.

But also aching.

Because even though she'd gotten to take home that heavy metal ring of gold, she hadn't been out there, eking out that win, scrumming on the ice, blocking shots, deking, shooting, scoring. She'd missed sharing the joy of earning that final win.

So, FOMO. Yeah, it was a real bitch.

The difference was that Calle had never held it against her teammates.

Unlike Jason.

He'd been happier when she was recovering from being injured than when she was playing, so attentive and caring and helpful that she hadn't recognized that particular mindfuck until just before they'd broken up, almost two years before.

Stupid? Probably. But she'd also been so busy with rehab and school that she'd been able to ignore a lot of their problems.

Then Jason had been in town, and he'd called being all sweet, and Calle had been lonely and . . . she'd had a moment of temporary insanity.

Fuck.

Why had she thought for a moment that he might have changed? That *this*—she placed her hand over her stomach—would change anything.

People didn't change.

So, now she had a useless prescription for birth control pills that had failed, a job where she worked with tough, strong men all day and where she needed to look tough and strong as well, and pretty soon she was going to be whale-sized, waddling down the hallway.

"Oh God."

She wanted to plunk her head back down onto her desk, to bang it a few more times for good measure, but she had to get ready for the game that night, which meant she had tape to watch, players to check up on, and line combinations to float by Bernard, the team's head coach. She also needed to check with the physical therapy staff and make sure there weren't any new restrictions for the athletes she wanted in the game that she didn't know about and—

Calle could not fall apart.

That was the most important thing.

Well, that and avoid Coop.

Coop.

Why of all of the Gold players and staff had she blurted out the truth to *him?*

They were the same age. They'd both grown up in Georgia, though their circles hadn't overlapped until now, mostly because Calle had been lucky enough to move to be part of a talented, albeit burgeoning, girl's program in Maine early and hadn't needed to play with the boys. This was unlike Brit—the team's starting goalie who was the first female player in the league. A few years older than Calle, she had played mostly on boy's teams.

What a difference those years had made, though. While Brit had needed to fight her way up through the ranks on all-boys teams, Calle had played with girls her age and older, had opportunities to play on the junior national and participate in training camps before proceeding to make the national team and competing internationally.

Brit had gone to juniors, to the AHL, and finally to the Gold.

And was one of the team's most talented and solid players.

She was who Calle should have blurted her troubles out to. *She* got what it was like to be a female in this industry, knew what it was like to deal with male players and their hang-ups and egos.

Brit had also handed many, *many* assholes their asses.

Calle should have taken notes before calling Jason.

But she'd thought—

"Ugh!" She pushed her chair back and shot to her feet. What was the definition of insanity? Doing the same damned thing over and over again? Well, then the last ten minutes of moping around in her office were fucking insane.

She was thinking herself in circles, wishing that the outcome of her conversation with Jason had been different, that she hadn't blurted out what was happening to Coop.

But it *wasn't* different, and she *had* blurted.

There wasn't any way to go back, and she needed to get her shit together and do her fucking job.

"Do your fucking job, Calle Stevens," she muttered.

Yes, she was talking to herself.

"You have fucking *got* this."

Yes, it was morphing into a pep talk.

"Suck it the fuck up and get your shit done."

Yes, it involved copious f-bombs, but that was hockey and really, the word fuck was the absolute best curse word around. Though asshole had a nice ring to it. Especially today. And douche canoe. That was always a good one.

See? Now she was distracted with thinking about the proper ranking order of curse words and not the problem in her uterus.

Problem—

Fuck.

Her heart spasmed, because no matter that the baby growing

inside her was the size of a strawberry—yes, she'd looked it up, right after taking the second test in the pack—she was already in love.

Already feeling protective.

Already imagining holding the precious little bundle in her arms and—

She'd always wanted kids. *That* wasn't the issue.

She had a good job with excellent health coverage. She owned a condo, had a car, even a savings account. Calle was capable of caring for a baby.

She'd always just pictured that the caring for a baby part would be shared.

"It's for the best," she murmured. Jason wasn't the partner she wanted to share parental duties with. Maybe she'd been hoping that initially, but the conversation they'd just had told her otherwise.

Such vitriol.

Accusing her of trapping him. Telling her to abort. Saying she wouldn't get a dime.

And all she'd been able to think was . . . strawberry.

That little strawberry growing inside her body was hers to protect and keep safe, hers to grow and love and—

No, she couldn't just get rid of it.

She needed a lawyer, to get him to sign his rights away, to make sure he never came back and—

No.

She needed a doctor's appointment. Calle needed to make sure everything was how it seemed, make sure her little strawberry was safe and well. She needed to cross her T's, dot her I's, have a plan of attack.

Her superpower was preparation.

This would be the perfect use of that skill.

She grabbed her tablet, shoved her cell into her pocket, and headed for the door.

Step one, find a doctor. Step two, talk to a lawyer, get Jason the fuck out of her life. Permanently. Step three, find Coop, swear him to secrecy. He wasn't prone to gossip much, not like the rest of the players, but she needed to make sure he didn't blab this around until her plan was in motion.

See?

She had this.

Although, maybe she should move step three up to step one. If Coop did say something . . .

She reached for the door handle, pressing it down and tugging the wooden panel open, mentally running through Coop's schedule and deciding where would be the best place to track him down. The weight room, probably. He always—

"Calle."

Heat down her spine, goose bumps prickling to life on her arms.

That warm, raspy voice had always been appealing.

Now it had gentled, softened, melted, coating her skin with honey. Her breath caught, her pulse accelerated, and her quads went a little shaky, as though she'd stayed out on the ice for too long of a shift.

She turned, stared up into the face of one of the most attractive men she'd ever laid eyes on. He was as gorgeous as Idris Elba, but even more so, because along with beautiful deep russet skin, intense eyes, and a strong jawline came all of the built yumminess of a hockey player's body—powerful thighs, narrow waist, totally grabbable ass.

But that attraction had always been tempered with professionalism.

On both their sides.

Well, Coop had always been professional. She'd pretended to be professional while surreptitiously giving into weakness and occasionally checking out his ass.

The point was, she'd been careful to keep a distance between them.

She was a coach. He was a player.

They weren't friends, *couldn't* ever be.

But now he knew something about her. Something big. Something that had changed their dynamic.

Because it wasn't careful distance in his gaze now.

His deep brown eyes were intense and for a heartbeat, it stole the air from her lungs.

"I—"

She didn't know what she'd been planning to say, because Coop stepped forward, cutting off her words and crowding her back into her office.

And she let him.

Because she was suddenly nose-close to the broad expanse of his gorgeous chest, the spicy tang of man assaulting her senses, becoming abruptly aware that aside from being the prettiest man she'd ever seen, he had extremely kissable lips.

He spun, giving her his back, and she had a millisecond to appreciate the sight of his shirt stretched tightly over his muscles before she heard it.

It being the *click* of the lock sliding home.

Coop turned back.

His mouth descended.

THREE

COOP

God, how could such a delicate face belong to such a fierce warrior on the ice?

Calle appeared slender, too thin to possibly be a force in the game, but Coop knew that her looks were deceiving.

Her face might be angelic, her body thin, but she packed a punch.

He knew from personal experience.

A few weeks ago, she had been demonstrating her technique for bodying someone off the puck to a few of the smaller players and had asked Coop to be her example of a big brute.

Her words, said with a beatific smile.

And fuck, he had just skated right over, all confident that she wouldn't be able to get the puck away from him, and totally missing the edge of mischievousness in her expression.

The technique was important.

The game was changing, and while no one would say the guys were small, there was a growing force of smaller-in-stature players on the team and in the league in general.

"I've never been the heftiest," she'd said, lips quirking as she'd nudged Coop in the back of his legs with her stick. "Not like this guy here. But we can be smart about where and how we apply pressure and try to win more of these battles." Her pretty brown eyes had lifted to his. "Ready?"

He'd grabbed the puck, turned partway toward the boards as she'd indicated.

Still over-confident.

Still laughing to himself that this tiny little waif of a thing in no pads was going to try to get the puck away from him.

"Rea—*fuck!*"

One second the puck had been on his stick, the next he was teetering back on his heels, fighting for balance while the puck was cradled on the blade of Calle's.

"That's physics," she'd said, lips curving. "They're a bitch."

Coop had snorted and regained his balance, ignoring his teammates, many of whom were laughing so hard *they'd* nearly fallen over, and thanking the hockey gods that the practice had been closed to the media. The hockey blogs would have eaten him up and spit him out because he'd been bested by a girl, no matter that Calle had proven herself to be a talented player time and again.

There were plenty of assholes in this world, and some of the sports bloggers definitely fell into that category.

Of course, many of his teammates also did.

Stefan, their captain, had lived with the shit-eating grin on his face for the rest of the day.

Brit had skated from the goal, dropped to her knees, and bowed down to Calle.

Blue, one of their most talented forwards, had gone so far as to have a shirt made up that just said, "Physics," and had left it in Coop's locker.

And Coop? He'd grumbled and glared, but he'd also . . . fallen in love.

Okay, not precisely. He'd already fallen for beautiful, angelic Calle approximately two minutes after seeing her—that being after Bernard had given her the floor at a team meeting and she'd diagnosed a problem with their offense as casually as if someone were choosing between Ranch and Caesar dressings on their salads.

Pretty, but smart as hell.

Talented, a smooth, efficient skater, even with the slight hitch in her stride that was the result of her injury, and thoughtful.

She was a cerebral coach but never seemed to get bogged down demonstrating or explaining those ideas, and she should have been a chess master for how many steps ahead she could think, how she seemed to be able to predict how the play was going to develop, even before the players themselves did.

A huge asset to the team.

And hands down, the most incredible woman he'd ever met.

That was huge, as the Gold crew was filled with a plethora of smart and talented women—Brit as their goalie, Rebecca as their nutritionist, Mandy their trainer, Bex as their publicist, not to mention that his mom had always been extremely capable and take-charge.

The difference between all of those women and Calle was . . . well, he didn't want to fuck any of them.

Calle, on the other hand—

All. The. Fucking. Time.

But they were both doing their jobs. The Gold might be ripe for inter-organization romances and their subsequent happily-ever-afters, but that same formula just didn't add up when it came to a player and a coach.

There was a power dynamic. A risk of being called out for favoritism.

He wouldn't do that to Calle.

Not to mention, he wouldn't ask a male coach out on a date, so he sure as fuck owed Calle the same courtesy. Yes, he'd fallen and fallen hard. Yes, he wanted her, but he also respected her and her job. So no, Coop wouldn't do anything to jeopardize that.

He'd flipped the switch in his mind—mentally ignoring how

fucking great it had been to have her pressed to his back, how sexy she looked in fucking track pants and a hoodie, not to mention those power suits she wore on game day—and put Calle firmly into the Not Female category.

They worked together and nothing more.

The technique had been successful for the last year and a half. Today?

He'd seen her as a woman again.

He'd seen those tears, had hated seeing her upset, and she'd been . . . vulnerable. So how in the fuck was he going to be able to go back and think of Calle as just his coach?

Coop had been weighing that as he'd gone back inside the arena, as he'd headed toward the weight room to get his work-out in.

But he'd gotten as far as the door to the Training Suite.

Mandy, their trainer, and Blane, a teammate, had been there, standing close together and loving on their daughter.

And he'd thought of Calle.

The way she'd sounded on the call, and her douche bag of an ex—and yes, Coop knew enough about Calle to know she'd dated Jason Marchand, an AHL player who was talented but would probably never make it in the NHL because he was a fucking pain in the ass. He also knew enough about Marchand after playing with him for a season to know he was a tiny-dicked fuckhead who didn't have half the smarts of Calle.

But that didn't change the fact that she was pregnant with his baby.

Coop had spun around in the hall, headed to her office, wondering all the while, if he should just leave well enough alone, if he should try to forget what he'd seen.

Even while knowing he wouldn't be able to.

So he'd kept walking and shown up just as she'd come out.

One glance at her face had told him all he needed to know.

He'd nudged her back inside, shut the door behind them, bent close and had opened his mouth to reassure her that he wouldn't say anything about the pregnancy, that he was here if she needed absolutely anything—

And then her lips had parted.

Lips that definitely didn't fit into the Not Female category. Lips he wanted to feel against his. Lips—

It took every ounce of strength he possessed to turn his head, but it was surprisingly easy to lift his arms, wrap them around her, and tug Calle against his chest. "I won't tell anyone," he murmured. "You don't have to worry."

She didn't say anything, and he might have dropped his arms and retreated, feeling like the biggest sort of asshole who'd over-stepped, if she hadn't shuddered out a breath and dropped her forehead to his shoulder. Her body relaxed against his, and yes, he was a perv for being all too aware of how good it felt to have her against him. But then she sniffed, and Coop forgot about all the urges he was stifling.

Instead, he stayed in place and rubbed his hand up and down her back.

It was the single most perfect experience of his life being able to be so close to Calle, smelling the slightly floral scent of her hair, feeling her lithe curves against his body, knowing that she was allowing him to hold her, to be this close.

Eventually, though, she exhaled and lifted her head.

"Sorry," she murmured, pressing lightly against the circle of his arms.

Coop dropped them. "Why are you apologizing?"

Her eyes lifted to his then fell to her tablet. "Because it's so incredibly unprofessional for me to have unloaded on you this morning and now"—she waved an arm between them—"I just had a meltdown in your arms."

The corner of his mouth tipped up. "*That's* what you consider a meltdown?"

Calle sighed and turned away, her long brown ponytail flying over one shoulder. "I'm . . . not on my game, Coop, and I need to get my head together. I appreciate you not telling anyone. But we've got a big matchup tonight. The team needs these two points to stay ahead of the Sharks and—"

And back to Not Female.

Back to strictly professional.

He understood that was what both of them needed to do, so Coop did what *he* needed, what *Calle* needed him to do.

Another step back, him reaching for the doorknob, tugging it open.

"I think the line combinations from the last game will really work well against their defense," he said, stepping into the hall.

Her expression evened out, the worry leaving, relief softening the edges of her eyes. "I agree," she said, tablet still in hand as she followed him into the brightly lit space, but when he thought she'd turn away, dismissing him completely, dropping them both back into that player-coach dynamic again, her voice dropped. "Thanks, Coop," she murmured. "For everything."

His heart skipped a beat. "No problem," he said, then added, "It'll be okay."

Her shoulders straightened, her chin came up. "Yeah. It will be." She lifted the tablet, started to turn away. "See you on the ice."

Coop watched her walk down the hall, trying to put her back into the Not Female category.

But his palms itched, still able to feel her beneath them, his nose was still filled with the scent of her hair, his chest burned where her body had been pressed to his, and his heart . . . well, that organ ached.

It didn't want Calle walking away from him.

And yet he had to watch her go anyway.

———

Coop kept his head down over the next few days.

He'd pushed how it felt to hold Calle in his arms to the back of his mind and had interacted with her exactly as he had before the revelation. So what if he was dreaming about her every night? That wasn't such a huge deal.

He occasionally dreamed about Bernard.

Though those dreams didn't usually include him in bed with the much older man.

So . . . he was losing it.

Good times.

He tossed his messenger bag over his shoulder, waved to the guys, and headed out.

"Coop, wait!" Brit rushed out into the hall, breathless, hair wet and hanging down her back.

"What's up?" he asked.

"We're getting burgers tonight. Want to come with?"

He lifted a brow. "Rebecca know about this?"

Brit smiled and nodded. "Cheat day."

"What time are you going? I've got a couple of errands to run, but if I finish on time, I'm game."

"I'll text you." She punched his shoulder lightly. "I know you like to do the lone wolf thing, but we do enjoy spending time with you off the ice." She leaned in, dropped her voice like she was imparting state secrets. "I don't know if you know this, but you're kind of cool."

He stifled a laugh. "Well, I don't know if *you* know this, but *you're* kind of a dork."

A nod, lips quirking. "Not untrue."

He grinned. "Thanks for the invite."

She waved, damp hair swinging behind her as she spun and disappeared back into the locker room.

This team was something else.

He'd played in the NHL for six seasons now, having worked his way up the ranks, but his three years with the Gold were a whole new experience. This team was a business, of course, a group of people who did their jobs and did them well, but it was more than that. It was a family—an awesome, sometimes nosy, but fun, caring tapestry of people tied together with a common goal.

Winning another Cup.

They had the crew to do it, too.

Solid roster, number one spot in the league, and a win only two seasons before. Coop had been picked up right at the trade deadline, had been able to hoist the Cup, but part of him had felt like he hadn't completely earned it.

Yes, he'd been there for the final stretch of the season and for the playoffs, but it wasn't quite the same as being a part of the team for the entire process.

He wanted *that*, to earn another Cup from start to finish, not just hop on the train halfway through.

Ego?

Yes.

But he was a professional athlete, so wasn't some ego to be expected?

Rolling his eyes at himself, Coop turned the corner for the exit and pushed out into the late afternoon sunshine. They were at the practice facility today, the parking lot filled with the familiar mix of players' cars and those belonging to the parents of the kids practicing in the facility's other rinks, but there was one car that immediately caught his attention.

Mainly because the small blue hybrid had its hood popped and Calle was standing in front of it, face grim, cell in her hand.

Coop warred with himself for exactly two seconds before crossing over to her.

"Hey," he said when he was within a few feet.

She startled, eyes jumping to his. "Coop."

"Everything okay?"

"Yup!" she said brightly.

He paused, glanced between the exposed engine and her face, which was adorned with an almost maniacal smile. "You sure?"

"Yup!" Somehow an even more chipper response.

"Well, is there a reason that your hood's open and you're

staring down at the engine like it's the key to solving the mystery of how our universe came to be?"

"Nope." Her smile grew.

All right then. Clearly, she didn't want him interfering. He started to turn away.

"Just looking for the battery," she said, voice edging toward desperate.

"Okay." A beat. "You need some help with that?"

She rocked back on her heels. "It's only, I need to get to . . . somewhere, and I can't be late and—" Breaking off, she shook her head. "No, I don't want to keep you. You've spent all morning on the ice and in the weight room, I'll just call a Lyft now and come back later to call my roadside service company."

"The battery on hybrids is usually in the trunk." He walked around the back of the car and popped the trunk. Ah. Yup, there it was, a panel that could be removed to access the battery.

Calle came around to stand by his side.

"It's here," he said.

She nodded.

"I'll give you a ride—"

Her hair flew around her face as she shook her head. "N-no, it's okay. I'll"—she held up her phone—"just call—"

Coop weighed his options. He could either argue with Calle —not likely to be successful, since she was as stubborn as he was—or he could attempt to take the matter in hand—which might still be unsuccessful and backfire, because . . . circling back to how much stubbornness was currently in this three-foot radius.

Still, he chose option two.

He snagged her cell from her hand, and while she was gaping at him in surprise, he grabbed her backpack from the open trunk.

"Anything else?" he asked.

"What?" Her eyes darted between the phone he'd shoved into his pocket and the backpack in his hand.

"Anything else you need at the moment?"

"Um . . ." Her mouth opened and closed a few times, brows drawn down into a cute little furrow. "No?"

"Cool." He shut the trunk, moved around to the hood and secured that, too, after which he retrieved the keys he'd spied sitting in the driver's seat. A glance over his shoulder told him that Calle was still standing by the now-closed trunk, her mouth slightly agape.

When she saw him glancing back at her, she visibly shook herself. "What are you doing?"

"Come on," he said, pocketing the keys and heading for his car.

"What?"

He stopped, turned back. "I'll drive you where you need to go. Later, I'll drive you back and you can call for a tow truck."

"No, that's—"

Another rotation. This time taking him back in the direction of his car.

"Coop."

He *bleeped* the locks on his car. "Didn't you say you were running late?"

Silence.

He climbed in, tossed the backpack behind his seat, and waited.

The passenger's side door opened, and Calle leaned in to glare at him. "This is beyond presumptive and bossy."

"And you're late."

More narrowed eyes in his direction. A long-suffering sigh.

Then she maneuvered herself into the seat and closed the door. He waited until she'd buckled in to ask, "Where to?"

And was glad that he had because it gave him a couple of seconds to lock the doors and start pulling out of the spot when she stiffened, reached for the handle, and said, "You know what? I'll—"

Then it was too late, unless she wanted to try her hand at tucking and rolling, because he was turning out onto the street.

"Hope I'm going the right direction," he said, cheerfully, choosing to go right.

She crossed her arms, sighed. "You are. I'm going to the doctor." She told him which hospital and clinic, and he nodded. It wasn't far off.

"Oh." He hesitated, wondering if he'd be a nosey asshole to press for details at this point. But then figured he'd already gone this far, so he might as well embrace his front row seat on the gossip train. "Everything okay?"

There. That sounded innocuous enough.

"With what?" she asked, reaching back for her backpack and pulling it into her lap.

Apparently, *too* innocuous.

"With you?" he asked.

She glanced up at him, brows assuming their cute little pucker for the second time in less than ten minutes. "With me?"

He sighed, slid the car to a stop as the signal turned red. "Yes, with you, *Calle*. You're going to the doctor. Is everything okay with you?"

"Yes." She'd unzipped her backpack, pulling out a spiral-bound notebook. "It's um . . . for the baby."

Ah.

The light turned green, and he pulled forward, not missing the fact that her gaze had already drifted down to the notebook in her lap, or the slight crinkle as she turned pages.

"Are you—?"

He stopped himself from asking something unforgivable. He'd already pushed her into accepting his help and he wasn't the baby's father, so he didn't have any right to ask the question that had been bouncing around in his brain. Apparently, he'd been around the guys and Brit in the locker room if he was willing to step over the polite, friendly conversation line and dare to ask Calle what she was planning to do with her body, with her pregnancy.

Her body. Her choice.

Even if the idea of her going through that made him a little sad.

She deserved to have everything she wanted, and someone to share it with.

Her eyes lifted from the notebook, met his, but thankfully, traffic began moving and he navigated his way through the intersection and onto the freeway.

"Am I what?" she asked softly.

"It's none of my business." he said quickly.

Silence, then, "*Now*, it's none of your business?" she asked. "After you all but forced me to get into your car?"

"Technically, you got in of your own accord."

"Did you forget the part where you took my phone and backpack?"

"No."

"And keys?"

"Didn't forget that either."

She huffed.

He concentrated on the road.

"I'm nervous," she said after a few minutes. "I'm going for my first appointment, and I'm worried the baby isn't . . . I don't know. That something is wrong, and I should have found out for sure before I called Jason."

His heart clenched. "Does something feel wrong?"

Out of the corner of her eye, he saw her shake her head. "No," she said. "I just started reading up on everything, and then I started seeing everything that could go wrong and . . ."

"You can't control it."

She closed the notebook, slipped it back into her bag. "I wrote down all of these questions, and I realized that the answers to none of them will matter if the baby is-isn't okay."

"It'll be okay."

"But how do you *know*?" She sighed. "Never mind, I know what you mean. It'll be okay or it won't, and there isn't much I can do about it. I'm along for this fucking ride I didn't sign up for, and I have to—"

He changed lanes, maneuvering around a slow truck. "Embrace the inevitable."

"Yeah, that," she said, but when he glanced over at her, her shoulders had relaxed slightly. "Also, I'm keeping it." Her voice was gentle. "I'm guessing that's what you were going to ask earlier but were too polite to actually finish the question." The side of her mouth he could see turned up. "I'm not mad. I'd probably be just as nosy if the situations were reversed."

"It's none of my business." He slid into the right lane, since the exit was coming up.

"Another season with the crew, and you'd have gone there anyway."

"Maybe," he admitted. There weren't exactly a lot of secrets in the Gold organization.

"Plus, I'm the one who blurted out the situation to you," she pointed out. "And it's not like I'm going to keep it a secret. I just . . . wanted to make sure things were okay first."

The off-ramp was backed up, so he had time to turn to her, to squeeze her arm. "It'll be okay, Cal," he said. "You're healthy and smart. I know you'll prep for this baby like you prep our offense, and you'll kick ass doing it."

"Thanks, Coop," she murmured. "And thanks for kidnapping me today so I wouldn't be late."

"Speaking of which"—he reached into his pocket and pulled out her cell—"here." Traffic started moving, and he spent the next few minutes navigating the road before pulling into the hospital's parking lot.

He pulled into a spot near a set of double doors leading into the OB-GYN clinic.

"I'll see you tomorr—"

"I'm coming in," he interrupted. "I'll sit in the hall and wait until you're done."

"Oh no," she began. "That's—"

"You're running late," he reminded. "And no one should have to be alone for this. At least not the first time."

She sighed, glanced down at her hands. "You're going to push this, aren't you?"

"I'll wait in the hall," he said instead of committing to that statement.

Another sigh, but instead of arguing, she just grabbed her backpack and said, "Only because arguing with you about this is going to make me later."

FOUR

CALLE

C oop was sitting in the waiting room. Not waiting in the
hallway.

This had occurred through a set of Murphy's Law
consequences that saw Calle rushing down the hall just as the
receptionist had come out to start closing up the office. She'd
taken one look at Calle's no doubt harried face and smiled.
"Don't worry, honey. You've made it. The doctor is still here and
running behind as usual. Come in, and I'll lock up behind you
guys. You can be the last of my stragglers sneaking in."

Coop had hesitated, assured confidence from the drive fading
at the sight of the female in pacifier-covered scrubs and the
intense floral motif they could glimpse in eye-aching clarity
behind her.

"Oh no," the receptionist said, noticing his uncertainty. "Boys
are allowed in nowadays. Just come in, grab some seats, and I'll get
the paperwork."

"I—" He started to turn, to point over his shoulder and—

The receptionist took his arm and in a series of moves that
impressed Calle to the marrow of her bone, effortlessly had

Coop's giant hockey player body through the door and into a chair.

The *click* of the lock had him jumping.

"Is this some horror film, and now we're going to die?" he asked, eyes wide. "What kind of doctor locks people in a room?"

"Oh, you're not locked in," the receptionist said cheerfully, tucking a strand of hair behind one year. "You can leave whenever you want. More people just can't get in."

"Oh." Coop's shoulders sagged in relief.

"Fill these out, honey," she said, handing a clipboard to Calle along with a pen.

"Doesn't feel great to be manipulated, does it?" Calle told him under her breath.

His face screwed up. "Is this your version of pot-meets-kettle?"

"It *is* the perfect life example," she pointed out.

He grunted. "And I didn't manipulate. I just . . ."

"Forced me to do what you wanted, even though I didn't?"

His face had drawn into a scowl, but as her words processed, it transmuted into guilt. "Shit, Calle. I'm—"

"Don't apologize," she said. "I'm teasing." Mostly. But he'd also been trying to do something nice and she didn't need to rub that guilt in. She squeezed his hand. "Thanks for getting me here on time. Let's leave it at that, okay?"

He nodded.

She sighed and glanced down at the clipboard. Honestly—and not that she'd admit this—but it would be kind of nice knowing that someone was out in the waiting room, at least minimally concerned about what was happening back in the exam room. She didn't have much of that anymore. Her mom had passed away just before she'd blown out her knee, and her dad . . . well, she supposed he had loved her, considering she was his flesh and blood. But he'd always been closer to his career and anyway, it wasn't like she could resurrect the dead to rebuild a relationship that never was.

The team was close, holding regular events that drew out most of the roster, and she did occasionally hang out with Brit, Mandy, both Rebeccas, and the rest of their crew. But a lot of the same dynamic existed between her and Brit as it did between her and the other members of the team.

Calle was hesitant to get too close in case someone called her out for favoritism.

It was at least slightly easier with Brit, since she wasn't involved in the decision of who played in net.

But offense was hers. She made the lines—with Bernard's final approval, of course. Yet, Bernard hadn't once disregarded her recommendations. He might offer a tweak here or there, but if she felt strongly about a particular combination, then he went with it.

And Coop was on offense.

So, even if there wasn't a conflict of interest from their power dynamic—she got to decide if he played and oftentimes how much and if he started—then there was at least some awkwardness with them being at her obstetrician's together.

She could imagine the headlines now.

Or, if not that, then she could definitely imagine the gossip train chugging right along the tracks.

Good grief.

"All set, honey?" the receptionist called, interrupting her thoughts and making Calle realize that she'd somehow filled out the forms without realizing. Quickly, she glanced back over what she'd written, was thankful that it made sense.

After pushing up to her feet, she returned the clipboard and pen then went back and sat down.

She turned to Coop. "You should probably go—"

"Calle?"

A door she hadn't noticed on the far side of the reception desk had opened. She popped back up to her feet.

"See you after," Coop said.

Torn between wanting to open the argument up again and

not wanting to keep the nurse waiting, she hurried across the room.

"Oh, your husband can come, too," the nurse said.

"H-he's not—"

She smiled. "Boyfriends are allowed in, too." The nurse glanced over Calle's shoulder. "Come on back, sir."

"I—"

"As soon as you get her in a room," the receptionist called to the nurse, talking over Coop. "go ahead and take off. I know you don't want to be late to get your Ethan from basketball practice."

The nurse smiled. "Thanks, Leanne." She gestured down the hall. "If you'll just follow me."

"Okay."

There was a slight scuff behind her, and Calle turned, saw Coop was now standing wide-eyed, the receptionist doing another one of those arm things, and suddenly he was directly behind Calle, the door to the waiting room *snicking* closed behind them.

"What kind of a monster is she?" he whispered.

"Just wait until I go into a room and then sneak out," she whispered back as they trailed the nurse to a scale.

"Good plan," Coop whispered back.

A minute later, the nurse had her weight and had shown them to an exam room. Calle sat on the paper-covered table feeling extremely uncomfortable at having Coop in the small space with her. He seemed too big, his bulky muscled form taking up all the space, sucking out the oxygen. Or maybe that was just because it was hard to ignore the effect he had on her when he was this close.

No. It was just her nerves.

She was unexpectedly pregnant by her jerk of an ex, and now she was trapped in a room where she was expected to get naked and flash what her mom had given her to the world at large.

Not that she would be doing that with Coop in the room.

The nurse would leave.

He'd slip out and—

"Good," the nurse said, typing a few things into the computer. "Your blood pressure and temperature are fine. You're starting at a healthy weight. Things are looking great." She set a paper gown and drape into Calle's lap. "I'll leave so you can change into these and the doctor will be right in."

"Thank you," Calle said.

The nurse smiled and went out the door.

Before it even closed completely, Coop was on his feet. "I'll meet you in the hall."

She nodded. "Go."

He reached for the door, but there was a knock from the other side, the wooden panel pushing open, forcing Coop to retreat. A woman in a white lab coat slid through the opening. "Oh!" she said. "I'm sorry. I didn't realize you hadn't changed yet. I'll just wait right outside while you do. Holler when you're ready."

The door closed.

Calle stared at it for a long moment then turned to Coop. "What do we do?"

"I don't know."

More staring, and if her expression was anything like his, then there was no shortage of horror to go around.

And meanwhile, the doctor was waiting out in the hall.

Shit. Fuck. Son of a donkey's behind.

"Turn around," she hissed.

He spun. She stripped and threw on the paper gown as quickly as humanly possible, lying back and using the drape to cover herself.

"Okay," she whisper-shouted and pointed toward the chair at her side. "Come up here so you're away from"—she waved her hand—"*there.*" He nodded, hurried to the chair, and she called out. "Ready!"

The doctor came through the door. "Hi, Calle. I'm Dr. Holdings." She held out her hand, and Calle shook it. "And you are?" she asked Coop.

His eyes cut to Calle's, and she shrugged.

He reached out and grasped the doctor's hand. "Cooper Armstrong, ma'am."

Dr. Holdings nodded. "Nice to meet you both," she said and turned back to Calle. "I know you came in for a blood test to confirm your pregnancy a few days ago"—she paused, and Calle nodded—"sorry I couldn't squeeze you in for an exam then."

"Oh, it's okay," Calle said. "I was just . . . nervous and wanted to know for sure."

Dr. Holdings smiled. "Sometimes it's hard to trust your faith to a drug store test."

"Yes, exactly that."

"Well, we'll get you sorted," Dr. Holdings said and slid a rolling stool over to the table. "Before you leave, though, I'll need a quick urine test. I knew you were waiting and didn't want you to have to wait to see and hear your little one."

"I can hear it?"

"Yes," Dr. Holdings said and pumped some hand sanitizer into her palms before pulling on a pair of gloves. "We'll take a quick ultrasound. We won't be able to see the baby's gender, but we should be able to hear your little one's heartbeat."

She sucked in a breath.

Shit was about to get real.

"I'm going to touch you on your abdomen now, okay?"

She glanced at Coop, but he had his gaze on his lap, so she nodded. "Okay."

The doctor began pressing different parts of her stomach, inching her hands lightly across her torso. "Did you have questions?"

She couldn't be certain, because she could only see the side of Coop's face, but Calle thought she could detect his mouth curving up from the slight crease in his cheek she could see on the side nearest her. In any event, her lips turned up in a smile because, hell yes, she had questions. "Only nearly a notebook's worth of them," she admitted.

Dr. Holding's didn't appear deterred. "Lob them at me," she said. "I'll continue with the examination. I'll need to do a pap smear and a breast"—Calle wasn't sure if the doctor heard Coop's strangled groan, but *she* certainly did—"exam and then we'll be able to take a listen to the baby. Sound good?"

Another glance at Coop. His gaze was still firmly on his hands. Mortification was a heavy blanket, and she knew her cheeks were red-hot. But what else could she say besides, "Okay."

Dr. Holdings spread the opening of the gown, Calle closed her eyes and was torn between silently wanting the exam to be over and knowing that a pap smear was going to involve an even more intimate part of her body exposed for the world to see. When she didn't immediately ask a question, the doctor began talking, running through the answers to some of the big questions Calle had written in her notebook. Her poking and prodding of Calle's breasts didn't take long, and then she'd moved down to the stool and settled herself in front of the drape.

"Scoot down until your bottom is on the edge," she said, talking Calle through the movements and helping her get her feet settled on the stirrups. "Now, you'll feel my fingers and here's the speculum. Sorry, I know it's cold. Ready?" Dr. Holdings glanced over the drape. "This will be a bit uncomfortable."

Yeah, pap smears weren't the most fun.

She nodded.

Dr. Holdings did her thing as Calle tried to hold back her wince. Scraping cells off an intimate part of her body didn't exactly feel great.

Coop's hand covered hers.

She gasped softly.

"Sorry," Dr. Holdings said. "Almost done."

But that wasn't what had made Calle gasp. Coop's hand was warm, a little rough, and had sent sparks all up her arm.

Turning her head, she saw that he'd finally lifted his gaze from his lap, deep brown eyes locked onto hers. "You okay?" he mouthed.

Her heart skipped a beat, and she nodded.

"All done," Dr. Holdings said then picked up a device that would have looked like a scarily intense dildo if not for the next question that passed through her lips. "Ready to hear your baby?"

Calle forgot about the wand, worry and excitement spiraling through her. "Yes."

Some pressure, a few buttons pushed on the machine, and then . . .

Whoosh-whoosh. Whoosh-whoosh. Whoosh-whoosh.

Wonder then fear. "Is it supposed to be that fast?"

Dr. Holdings smiled. "Yes," she said. "It's right on track at 165 beats per minute. And considering you're ten weeks along, that's just perfect." She turned the machine so the screen faced Calle's direction. "And . . . *there's* your baby."

"Oh, it *is* a baby," Calle whispered, inanely, she knew, but she also hadn't expected it to look like *that*, like an actual baby with a head and arms and legs and . . . yes, she'd done research, yes, she'd read up—

But *no*, nothing could compare to actually seeing *her* baby on the screen.

Her throat went tight.

"Wow," Coop said, and she looked over at him, saw his eyes glued to the screen. His hand was still covering hers, and it squeezed lightly.

"I'll print a few pictures of the baby," Dr. Holding said softly.

Coop's stare drifted away from the screen, coming up to meet Calle's. Their eyes locked and held and . . . something deep and meaningful passed between them. New life or life changed or perhaps, simply the absolute astonishment in bearing witness of something so magical.

She swallowed hard, blinked rapidly, and his hand slipped from hers.

The pulse of disappointment she felt at the loss of contact was insane.

That wasn't up for discussion at this moment—

Coop's thumb brushed along her cheek.

Her breath hitched, and she realized that he'd wiped away a tear, but just as quickly as her mind caught up to his action, her eyes processed his expression.

Soft. Warm, mahogany eyes. Gentle smile.

She bit her lip, heart skipping a beat. He leaned closer, and—

Rip.

The tearing sound made them both jump.

"Sorry," Dr. Holdings said, holding up a strip of ultrasound snaps before handing over to Calle. The paper was thin and a little slippery, but the slightly blurry black-and-white images already meant everything. "Okay, so that's all done," the doctor said as she stripped off her gloves and stood. "How's the nausea?"

Calle shrugged. "There, but mostly in the mornings and manageable."

"All right," Dr. Holdings said. "Let me know if that changes, but ginger ale and saltine crackers are probably going to be your best friends for a little while." Calle nodded. "Now tell me, what other questions do you have?"

In one fell swoop, Coop slid the pictures from Calle's hand and swapped them for her notebook.

When he'd even taken it out of her backpack, she didn't know. What she *did* know was that her heart did that skipping-a-beat thing again and her stomach had gone all squishy.

"Thanks," she murmured.

He nodded encouragingly.

She opened the cover on the notebook and began rattling off the questions.

Dr. Holdings sat next to her, patiently answering everything Calle threw at her: Was it safe to eat lunch meat? Yes. What about coffee? In moderation, fine. What kind of medications should she avoid? Ibuprofen, aspirin, and several other types often used for coughs and colds. Acetaminophen was the safest bet.

Then the most important question: could she still be on the ice with the guys?

She held her breath as she waited for the answer, knowing that if she couldn't, then coaching was going to get a lot harder . . . as well as potentially keeping her job.

"For now, yes," Dr. Holdings said. "Many women continue their normal activities up to their due date."

Relief poured through her.

"Although—"

Her stomach tightened.

"You're not working out with the team or involved in the actual games, right?"

Calle shook her head. "For the most part, no. I'm on the bench during games, and not on the ice for warmup or anything like that. During practice, I'll occasionally demonstrate something, but aside from that, there's nothing really physical, so it's not like one of the guys is going to check me into the boards or I'm going to rip a slapshot."

"Okay." A nod. "So, for now, let's continue on as you've been doing. Once the baby gets bigger—along with you—you'll probably need to make some accommodations to being on the ice so that you don't become a fall risk." She picked up an electronic tablet and typed in a few notes. "We'll revisit this in your second trimester."

Calle relaxed. "Sounds good."

"What about if she gets hit with a puck?" Coop asked. "Or someone falls and cuts her with a skate blade?"

Dr. Holdings frowned. "Has that happened?"

"No," Calle said.

"Yes," Coop said at the same time.

One of Dr. Holdings' brows lifted.

"Well," Calle admitted. "It *has* happened, of course. In the history of hockey, people have gotten hit with pucks or sliced with skates. But those are players and not coaches, for the vast majority. I can definitely take precautions," she said. "But I need my job, and these guys are insanely talented. They can skate while controlling a puck better than most of the rest of us walk down the sidewalk."

Coop made a noise and when she glanced over at him, she saw his face had gone dark, thunderclouds filling his expression.

Thankfully, Dr. Holdings began talking. "Got it. For now, this seems like a lower risk than some of my other patients, so let's just take it one day at a time, and we'll reevaluate in a month." She set the tablet down. "That being said, if at any point you feel uncomfortable with what you're doing, then *stop* doing it."

Calle smiled. "I can do that."

"Good." The doctor smiled back then turned and pulled out some fliers and samples from a drawer. Next, she wrote out a prescription for prenatal vitamins and stuck everything into a bag. "I think we're good here. Don't forget to leave a urine sample before you go—instructions are in the bathroom. Just use the facilities, bring your sample to the deposit box at the end of the hall, and we'll call if there's an issue." She took a step toward the door. "In the meantime, you're healthy and it looks like you two are prepared with questions and concerns. Keep staying on top of it and you'll breeze through this."

"Thank you," Calle murmured.

"Thanks, Doc," Coop said

With a wave, Dr. Holdings left, the door shutting behind her with a soft *click*. Neither she nor Coop moved, and silence descended.

Then he stood. "I'll—uh—wait in the hall?"

Her head bobbed up and down. "Yes, please."

He'd snagged the notebook from her lap, picked up her backpack, and disappeared into the hall almost before the two words passed her lips.

Then there was one.

She glanced down at the pile of clothes next to the table, at her paper-and-fabric-covered body, and took a moment to ponder what in the fuck all had just happened.

Her baby's heartbeat.

Cooper.

Her practically naked and spread eagle on a table.

In front of Cooper.

Yeah, that seemed to be the most important common denominator.

"Oh my God," she muttered, mentally smacking herself into motion. She slid down from the table, reached for her clothes, and began to get dressed. How the last hour had managed to shake down, she wasn't sure she'd ever fully process, but it *had* happened, and she'd shared it with Coop.

With Coop.

Coop.

She'd been almost naked, her lady bits exposed to the room, her breasts examined, and a speculum—

Fuck her life.

This might be the most embarrassing thing that had ever happened to her.

She yanked up her pants, tugged her Gold sweatshirt over her head, and saw the container Dr. Holdings had left on the counter.

"Oh fuck," she groaned.

Scratch the *might be* part of her thinking.

She'd forgotten she got to add to her embarrassment by carrying a jar of her own pee down the hallway in front of Coop to her experience.

Might be was out. Definitely the *most* embarrassing event of her life.

Kudos to her for exceeding her own expectations.

FIVE

COOP

"Thanks," Calle said when he handed over her backpack. They'd had a slight scuffle over the bag after she'd emerged from the bathroom, but thankfully, the receptionist had used her magical powers to detect their brewing argument and had popped her head out to schedule Calle's follow-up appointment.

He'd taken the opportunity to escape into the hall, still carrying her backpack.

Though, not before he'd made a mental note of the date.

Just in case.

Now, she was back in his SUV and they needed to sort out her car.

He rounded the hood and opened his driver's side door, but before he got in, he noticed there was some dirt on the floor mat. So, in a move he'd done hundreds of times since he'd finally made enough money to buy a nice enough car, Coop whipped the mat out.

One quick shake got the dust off and twenty seconds later, he had the mat secured.

Keys in the ignition, ass in seat, belt across his lap and chest, and secured.

Only then did he realize Calle was staring at him, mouth agape. "Oh my God," she said, shoving her backpack into the space at her feet. "It's true, isn't it?" Her lips tipped up. "I thought it was just the guys trying to find something they could tease you about, but it's actually true."

Aw shit.

He'd given Max, one of their defensemen, a ride home last season and had stopped the other man mid-potato chip consumption—a.k.a. Max doing his damnedest to grind every tiny crumb into the seams of Coop's leather seats.

Totally reasonable, he'd thought.

But it had given Max—and the team—the fodder with which to tease him about being obsessed over his car.

And look, he was a *tad* bit obsessed.

He liked his car clean. He liked things in their place. He hated feeling tiny, pokey crumbs under his ass when he wore shorts in his car almost as much as he hated having any visible trash in the SUV he'd worked really fucking hard to pay for.

Yes, with his new contract he could buy a new vehicle, one undoubtedly nicer and more expensive than this one.

But it wouldn't be *this* one.

"I don't know what you're talking about," he said, pushing the button to start the ignition and backing out of the stall.

"Coop."

He flicked his eyes in her direction.

"You just shook imaginary dust out of your floor mat."

"It wasn't imaginary—" Clicking his teeth closed to cut off his protest came too late. Calle's expression had already gone all cat-ate-the-canary.

"So, what do you do when it rains? Dry your baby gently with a three-hundred-thread-count silk towel?"

Actually, he used a ridiculously expensive chamois he'd picked up at a car show.

"I think there's a fingerprint on your nav screen."

His stare darted there.

Calle burst out laughing.

He sighed.

"I can't wait to tell the guys this."

Another sigh as he drove out of the parking lot.

"If you shaved your head, we could call you Mr. Coop."

"Yeah, no."

"But you'd look so cute bald and with one earring."

No. No, he would not.

She giggled, and even though it was the result of her giving him shit, it still made Coop feel like a million bucks. Seeing her smile like that, as though just teasing him had made some of the boulders she'd been carrying on her shoulders fall away, and he could have sworn he'd grown five inches and put on twenty pounds of muscle.

It made him feel invincible.

Fuck, she was special.

"I'm not getting an earring," he said, playing along.

"So, you're saying that shaving your head is not out of the question."

He pulled the car to a stop at a signal. "Have you seen my head? It looks like an egg." A shudder. "I shaved my head once, and the results weren't pretty."

"Pictures or it didn't happen."

"You're persistent."

"There *is* a reason I've made it as far in this industry as I have." She giggled again. "Though I'm guessing there's a reason *you've* made it this far, too."

"Persistent meet stubborn?"

"If the shoe fits."

Coop hadn't realized he'd been staring at her, entranced by the playfulness, loving how relaxed she seemed now that the appointment was over, and everything was okay and . . . she was fully clothed.

Well, there was that.

But anyway, he'd been watching her face change, studying the lines of her brows as they lifted and fell while she talked, the corners of her lips dancing as she fought a smile, the barest hint of a dimple appearing and disappearing on her cheek, and he'd been absolutely mesmerized.

At least until the horn blared behind them.

Coop's gaze shot forward and he hit the gas, sliding through the intersection as the light changed from yellow to red.

"Whoops," Calle said.

He chuckled.

"So, Mr. Coop is out," she murmured.

"That's a certainty."

"Bummer," she said and fell quiet as he continued down the road and pulled onto the freeway. "I should call Triple A," she murmured, a few moments later. "Get a jump on the wait time."

"Good idea."

But as she reached into her backpack for her cell, her stomach rumbled, the noise all but blaring like a siren through the quiet car.

"Maybe we should eat first?" he suggested.

"Oh, no," she said. "I can wait. You've already taken enough time out of your day."

"I'm hungry, too."

"Coop. *No.*"

He bit back a sigh. Although . . . one benefit of being in the driver's seat when a stubborn female sat in the passenger's seat meant he had control of at least one thing.

He took the exit for the practice rink . . . then turned in the opposite direction of it.

"What—?"

There was a cool outdoor space just around the corner, specialty markets mixed in with a variety of food stalls to fill the pavilion. One, in particular, he knew Calle was a fan of—Sam and Cheese—made gourmet dishes with, no surprise, plenty of cheese.

"Brie, cranberries, and apricot jelly, right?" he asked, navigating his SUV into a parking spot on the street across from the market.

"Coop—"

"On toasted sourdough bread?"

Her stomach growled again, but despite that, she shook her head again.

"Come on," he said. "It's my cheat day. I'm starving, and I need a brownie from Molly's stand."

Recently expanded into a restaurant spot in the Gold Mine, Molly's was a local restaurant that sported an awesome bakery, homemade soups, sandwiches, and salads, and was singlehandedly the reason he'd gained five pounds soon after moving to San Francisco.

It had been a lot easier to put them on than taking them off, that was for damn sure.

Calle sighed.

"Melted cheese, tart cranberry compote, homemade sourdough—"

She popped the passenger's side door, shoved out onto the sidewalk. "Fine," she bit out, grabbing her backpack. "What are you auditioning for the Food Network now?"

He smothered a smile as he got out on the driver's side, meeting her at the back of his car. They let a car pass then jay-walked across the road and moved into the open-air market.

"Sam and Cheese first?"

She grunted.

Sam and Cheese first.

They made their way over to the counter, ordered at the window—brie and cranberry grilled cheeses for both of them, since he'd heard Calle and Brit rave about the sandwich for long enough that he needed to try it for himself, and some of their homemade lavender and honey lemonade. He paid—ignoring her protest and taking advantage of the fact that he was taller, had longer arms, and had prepped by getting his wallet out, already anticipating the battle. "You can buy me a brownie."

Her expression went thunderous, and she sucked in a huge breath.

Coop braced himself.

Then she released it with a long, slow hiss of air. "Not exactly a fair trade," she said. "Be prepared for twenty dollars' worth of brownies."

"I'll take that trade." He grinned. "Especially when it's Coach giving the means to really take advantage of my cheat day."

"Fuck," she muttered.

He grinned, knowing the battle was mostly won. "I won't set Rebecca loose on you, I promise."

A roll of those pretty chocolate eyes. "Fine. I'll buy you one brownie, with the promise of another on the next scheduled cheat day."

"Deal."

Their nutritionist, Rebecca, had put together a great meal plan for the team. They had transitioned the players to a wholly vegetarian diet, with the bulk of their protein choices coming from plant-based sources. Some came from fish, eggs, milk, and cheese, but most often he stayed away from anything that came from animals . . . and he found that he didn't miss meat all that much.

Cheese, on the other hand?

That was hard to give up.

His mom's mac and cheese, cheddar biscuits, grilled cheese sandwiches, cheesecake—

Yeah, the dairy component was hard to keep in moderation.

So, he tended to stay away from it all and then go crazy on cheese—*cough*—cheat days.

And thank fuck he'd never let his nickname for the team's days off their diet plan slip in the locker room. The shit-givers would *love* to have something new to tease him about.

Although now Calle had car fodder.

"There it is," she said, and Coop blinked, realized he'd been wool-gathering while staring at the pickup window. He turned to face her.

"Sorry, what?"

Her cheeks went pink. "It's ridiculous."

"Well, I think we've had plenty of ridiculous today. Hit me with it."

Her face screwed up and she lifted a hand, tugged at the end of her ponytail. "It's just easy to tell, even from the side, when you smile."

He paused. Coop wasn't much for primping in front of the mirror, but he liked to think that he had slightly better than average looks. But maybe he was delusional and his smile really did make him look possessed like his older brother had always said.

Hockey players don't smile, Coop, Brendan had told him when he'd seen his first promotional pictures when Coop had finally made an NHL team. *You look like a pussy flashing all those pearly whites. You're supposed to be missing teeth by the time you make it to the big leagues.*

I paid a lot of money for that smile, his mom had chimed in. *So, no, he's not.* Then she'd smacked Brendan on the back of the head and had told him to never use that word—meaning pussy—in front of her.

Brendan hadn't.

Instead, he'd switched pussy to possessed when their mom was around, taking it so far as to say that he could see the devil in Coop's eyes when he smiled.

Asshole.

But also . . . heh.

He'd gotten Brendan back, though—sending him a sexy devil singing-gram to the fire station where his brother worked.

Those guys could razz as good as the players on the Gold.

Fuck, he needed to go home.

He missed his pain-in-the-ass sister, though she was closer

now, having recently moved to San Diego, and his parents. He even missed his brother. But also, Coop missed just being in the neighborhood where he'd grown up in Atlanta. Not that his current situation was bad. San Francisco was pretty great, too, and living out his dream of playing professional hockey was doubly so.

But it wasn't home.

"Why do you look like you swallowed a rotten egg?" Calle asked.

He shrugged, brushing off the homesickness, the little twinge of doubt it came from thinking about his smile and his brother's teasing. "No reason."

"Coop—"

Thankfully, at that point, the guy from Sam and Cheese called their number and Coop was able to escape before he said something along the lines of, "My big brother says my smile looks possessed, is it true?" or "I miss my mommy and want to go home."

"Should we grab a table?" he asked when he came back, paper trays of food and drink carrier balanced in his hands.

Calle nodded and led the way to a picnic table.

The sun was going down, the strings of lights crisscrossed overhead had turned on, and because it was a weeknight, the space wasn't too crowded.

In fact, it felt cozy and a little intimate.

Well, not more intimate than being in the same room as she'd undergone the exam, as stripping down with his back turned, and all sorts of scary-looking medical instruments put in—

"I've always liked how you smile with your whole face," she said.

Coop jerked his head up. "What?"

Her eyes were soft. "It's what I meant before. It's just . . . you have a great smile."

"I—uh—" He fumbled with his sandwich, gaze darting to hers and away.

"Have I struck the unflappable Cooper Armstrong mute?"

she asked, head tilting to the side, ponytail swinging out behind her, skin glazed golden by the lights above them.

And fuck, she was the most beautiful woman he'd ever seen.

"I never thought I'd see the King of the Soundbite at a loss for words."

His cheeks felt hot, and there was something about this woman, some special Calle Stevens magical fairy dust that made him feel about twelve years old again. And like a twelve-year-old, he also had all the smoothness of sandpaper. Which was why he blurted, "My brother says I look possessed when I smile."

Her brows drew down.

Oh, for fuck's sake.

He shoved his sandwich into his mouth, took a huge bite. Partly because it was delicious, but mostly because he needed something to shut him the fuck up.

She reached across the table and snagged a cranberry that had fallen into the paper tray, plucking it up between thumb and forefinger and sliding it between a set of lush lips that made his cock twitch. He was reeling from revealing too much, his cheeks burning, and Calle Stevens still gave him a hard-on.

Yeah, she had fucking magical fairy dust all right.

"I think you have a very nice smile," she said in between bites. "So many of the guys try to do this tough guy bullshit in the team photos, and I'm like I've seen you scream like a hyena when Max hides somewhere and jumps out at you." A grin. "So no, you're not that tough, you're a giant teddy bear, and I like that you don't try to pull something over in the publicity photos."

"PR-Rebecca would not agree."

She shrugged. "Probably not, but that's why she gets paid to do the PR and I get paid to help you guys play . . . and sometimes that's by keeping the egos in check."

PR-Rebecca was a media-spinning genius and the two Rebeccas together—PR and Nutritionist—along with Mandy, Calle, and Dani, meant the team's support staff was both diabolical in their planning ahead (and ego-checking) skills as well as totally kickass.

"I imagine the ego portion of the job gets to be a lot," he said.

"You'd imagine right," she said, tone teasing. "You know those professional athletes are so fragile."

"Definitely."

She did that head-tilt thing again, but her eyes had gone soft. "Why do I think that you looking possessed isn't the full story?"

"Why do *I* think that you're the one who told Max about his new hiding spot?"

"Why did *I* enjoy you jumping about six feet off the ground when he scared you?"

"Why did you bust out laughing when *everyone* jumped six feet off said ground?" he asked. "Well, everyone except Brit, because she's apparently got nerves of steel and is never scared or bothered by Max's pranks."

Aside from not jumping out of her skin when he popped out of random places, she'd not even batted an eye when Max had pasted her prom pictures—with Blane as her date (long story, but they'd grown up together, with Blane being madly in love with Brit until he'd gotten together with Mandy and realized that he and Brit would have never actually worked).

The fact that her fluorescent pink dress and their tough-as-shit goalie wearing about a pound of makeup and heels that matched had been plastered over every available inch of the locker room hadn't fazed her in the least.

She'd shrugged, said, "Cool."

Just *Cool*.

Then had gotten dressed.

See? A total BAMF.

As in, Brit was a badass motherfucker.

"Or . . . she has advanced intel."

A BAMF who apparently had inside information. He narrowed his eyes at Calle, demanded, "Who?"

She snagged another cranberry. "I never divulge my sources."

He scowled. "Angie," he accused.

Angie was Max's other half and Mandy's sister. Mandy was tight with Brit.

Calle just looked at him with an innocent expression he wasn't buying for a single minute.

"Traitors," he muttered. "The lot of you."

She snorted. "The *lot* of us?" she asked. "I think you mean the small but merry band of women who keep the ship on track and have had to band together against the cloud of egos and masculinity?"

His gut sank.

He reached for her hand. "Shit," he said. "Is it really that bad? I thought that since the organization was moving toward fifty-fifty men to women for the support staff that things had gotten better. Who's—"

"I don't need you to fight my battles, Coop," she said. "There is still some work to be done, people who aren't thrilled to be coached by a 'girl' or play with one, but I'm a grown woman and can handle my own shit." A pause. "As can Brit. And the rest of our posse."

Putting aside the term *posse* for the moment, he tried to pinpoint exactly who was giving her a hard time. Most of the guys had reserved judgment on Calle when she'd initially been hired, a few had been very hesitant in accepting coaching from someone who played a different version of the game. Women's hockey had contact, but no checking was allowed. That wasn't to say it didn't happen and the games between the US and Canada were particularly physical, but just as the men's game was starting to move toward speed and away from a plethora of bone-jarring, and potentially CTE causing hits, the women's game was much more about transitions, team play, and puck movement. Which were right in the Gold's wheelhouse—they generally had smaller, quicker players, and less of the enforcer-led play that had dominated the game he'd watched growing up.

So, Calle had the gameplay experience, but she was also able to transform that into information and suggestions the guys could easily pick up.

Which meant that any reticence had quickly transmuted into respect the previous season.

Still, Coop knew there had been a bit of a learning curve after training camp this year, a few of the younger guys who'd been picked up weren't used to either a female in the locker room or one giving them orders. Luckily, Bernard—their head coach—had absolutely zero patience for bullshit on a good day. And having one or more of his players questioning his assistant coach had not, in fact, made for a good day.

Asses had been chewed.

Calle had kept doing her thing.

The players had removed their heads from said chewed asses and things had gelled.

Or maybe they hadn't?

"Who—?"

She stood, grabbed their empty paper trays. "Brownie time."

"Call—"

But she was already walking toward Molly's food stand. He hurried to catch up with her, taking the trays from her hands and tossing them into the trash.

"Who's—"

"Stop," she snapped, whipping around to face him.

He froze, the tone far colder than anything he'd heard from her before.

"Look," she said, still frosty, "I appreciate you stepping in today, but I don't need a hero or someone to save me."

"I—"

"I've been on my own for long enough that I know how to take care of my shit, and I *certainly* know how to deal with men who don't think I know as much about hockey as them. There aren't many on this team, but occasionally one will let loose, and I can handle it. Okay?" She sucked in a breath. "What I *don't* need is you fucking up my job because you saw me in a situation that is decidedly *un*-coach-like and think that it means I'm going to fall over myself just because I said you have a nice smile and we hung out for a few hours."

The words clocked him across the face, stinging like he'd been sucker-punched. But, look, he got it. Circumstances meant that Calle had needed to prove herself, that sometimes she still needed to.

Fucking sucked that was her reality.

But the world was the world, and while most of those in their circle were cool, she couldn't control every asshole in the league.

Which meant she needed him to be cool *now*.

To let her handle her own shit.

To not get protective and overstep just because when he'd heard that heartbeat on the ultrasound machine, stared at the tiny human on the photographs the doctor had printed, Coop had felt . . . moved.

As though a piece inside him had shifted.

Because it was fucking magic and beautiful and amazing and fragile . . . and it was inside Calle.

But she didn't need him to think about magic.

She needed him to think about hockey.

About the team.

About her job.

"Calle—"

She didn't let him get out that he understood where she was coming from, that he would shut up and allow her to buy him a brownie, then he'd take her back to the rink. Nope. She didn't let him get *any* of that out.

Instead, she let loose on him.

"Fucking stop, Coop," she snapped. "I know all about men like you. They come on tough and sweet and strong, pretend to care, pretend to be protective." Her inhale and exhale were as sharp as her next words. "But the trouble with men, especially with supposedly protective and sweet and strong men, is that it's all *fucking bullshit*. You don't really mean it. You pretend to protect, just long enough to worm your way into our lives and fuck things up and—"

He'd heard enough.

He was not *that* guy, and he certainly wasn't anything like Jason fucking Marchand, as she was implying.

Coop leaned close, near enough to smell the lightly floral scent of her shampoo, near enough to see her eyes darken, near enough to smell the cranberry on her breath. "Forgetting for a second that you're lumping me in with that piece of shit you let shoot his load between your legs, you should know *me* well enough by now to understand that I don't pretend at *anything*." He leaned closer, heard her inhale sharply. "It's why I fucking smile in the promo pictures, why I tolerate Max's bullshit jokes, why I've given everything I have to this team." Closer still. "And that's just the team. The job. Because in my outside life, in the real fucking world, if it were *my* woman who was carrying *my* tiny, perfect baby in her belly, I sure as shit wouldn't be halfway across the US, doing fuck knows what in a career I didn't have a chance at advancing. I would have sorted my shit and been in that chair, in *that* room, watching with fucking tears in my eyes as I saw my baby for the first time."

Her lips parted, and he saw her eyes go damp. "Coop—"

He nodded at the stand. "Get your brownie if you want," he said, not looking at her. "I'll be in the car."

Six

CALLE

Well, the drive back to the rink had been glorious.

Gloriously awkward, that was.

And perhaps because she was a glutton for punishment or maybe because she was just lonely and realized she had unfairly unloaded on the only man who seemed to give a shit about her in her life of late, she didn't call Coop up to apologize when she got back to her condo.

Instead, she sent Jason a text.

Saw the doctor today.

Along with the bland statement, she sent over a snap of the ultrasound. More being a glutton. More punishment. More idiocy.

Because his response was pure Jason.

Asshole, succinct, and crystal clear.

Either get rid of it or send me whatever papers you need to. I'm out.

Not unexpected.

Still hurt.

"Dumb ass," she muttered, setting down her cell and wiping the back of her hand over her cheeks, brushing away the tears that had escaped unbidden. She would not waste her tears on that asshole. Plus, "What did you expect?"

Nothing.

She expected nothing from the men who'd been in her life.

It was so much easier that way.

Sighing, she got up and snagged an apple from the fridge, making short work of slicing it and scooping up a spoonful of peanut butter to go along with it. Coop had been true to his word, waiting in the car while she'd bought two brownies. Not for her. She'd been an ass and didn't deserve brownies.

But she knew that Coop had a weakness for cheesecake, so after watching him storm off, after the guilt of taking the easy camaraderie they'd developed over the last two years and shredding it to pieces with her unnecessary explosion had swelled within her to overfilling, she'd seen the special of the day was a cheesecake-swirled brownie and had bought him two.

Yes, she'd been freaking out about the way the intimacy had seemed to grow between them as the hours passed, but he didn't deserve her ire. He'd been nice, albeit a little pushy, but he'd stepped in, taken everything in stride, and made sure she'd gotten what she needed—whether it was to the doctor's or food or back to the rink so she could call Triple A to come fix her car.

And though, on the way back to the rink he hadn't spoken much more than in single-word replies and grunts, and she'd all but fled the tense atmosphere that was filling his SUV to make the call then sat in her own car to wait, Coop *still* hadn't left.

He'd waited until the tow truck had come, until the new battery was installed, until she was buckled in, her engine started, and until she was pulling out of the spot before he'd turned on his SUV and followed her out.

All the way to her condo south of the Gold's practice facility.

In the complete opposite direction of where he needed to go, since she knew he lived in the city.

"Ugh," she muttered, stomping to the kitchen and scooping out another spoonful of peanut butter.

She was going to get fat. She might as well embrace it by eating her favorite foods. And while Coop might have a sweet tooth and be obsessed with all things cheese and cheesecake-related, Calle loved peanut butter.

A spoon of it straight out of the jar.

Peanut butter M&Ms.

Peanut butter cups.

Peanut—

Well, the point was that peanut butter was her happy place, and after the day she'd had, after the text she'd just received, she deserved a little happy.

The only good thing about the whole situation with Jason was that she wasn't surprised about his reaction, and the timing was such that because the team had a game tomorrow night, there wasn't any practice in the morning, aside from an optional morning skate.

So, she'd already made an appointment with her lawyer.

Loads of fun for a rare weekday morning free.

"Too bad I couldn't get into the doctor tomorrow," she muttered, shoving the food in her mouth so the words came out garbled. Luckily for her, she was talking to herself, so the words in her head already made sense because . . . well, they'd been in her head.

Snorting, she scooped out another spoonful—and forget lecturing her about double-dipping, this was her personal jar of scooping peanut butter. She had a separate jar for company.

Not that she got a lot of company.

Not that she was going to lie and say the company jar of peanut butter didn't sometimes become her second personal jar of scooping peanut butter.

But a girl had to live, right?

Considering her mouth was all but sealed shut from the delicious, sticky concoction, Calle screwed the lid on, put the jar back on the shelf, dropped the empty spoon into the sink, and then headed back into the family room.

She called it that loosely, since her living space was basically one large room with a kitchen tucked into one corner, a battered, round table and chairs she'd scooped up from a neighbor's yard sale in the other, and her ridiculously expensive, but insanely comfortable couch taking up a third. The front door was between her "family room" and kitchen and looked directly into the short hall that led to the bathroom and two bedrooms.

Her condo wasn't luxury by any means, but it was newly built, backed up to some nice hiking trails, and it was hers.

The first piece of property she'd been able to afford to buy instead of renting. Funny story, women's hockey didn't pay a whole lot, but she'd been lucky enough to be on the squad when they'd received equal compensation to that of their male national team counterparts.

Used to living on a shoestring budget, or working another job while training, the pay increase had meant she'd been able to focus on playing.

Although, she *had* missed her day job.

Running the hockey programs for kids at a local rink as well as coaching a few of the teams there.

Practice plans for corralling thirty four-to-six-year-olds on the ice—all of whom were armed with sticks and had skate blades with varying degrees of sharpness strapped to their feet—were her specialty.

They'd been great.

More exhausting than her own practices, sometimes, but great.

And her connections meant that when she'd blown out her knee—shredding through her ACL and MCL in a major tear that had required three surgeries and still didn't feel quite right—she'd had something to fall back on.

By the time she'd rehabbed, someone had taken on her role at the rink, so she'd begun coaching a few local travel and high school teams. Then a friend of a friend had recommended her for a local college. She'd spent a season with the college, then one with the Gold's AHL affiliate, before Bernard had asked her to fill the shoes of their former offensive coach, Todd, who'd gotten a chance to be a head coach in North Carolina.

So now, instead of renting a room or a shitty apartment, she could afford to buy.

And thank God she'd gotten a place with two bedrooms.

She'd warred with herself over the decision—it wasn't like she had family who'd visit. Her parents were gone, her siblings scattered and well-established in their own lives.

Two bedrooms had been an added and unnecessary expense.

Now, she was glad she'd fallen in love with the sunny, corner unit and had splurged.

It would mean more room when the baby came.

When the baby came.

Oh God.

She was having a baby.

Why it really sunk in at that moment didn't make any logical sense. She'd peed on the stick and seen the plus sign, then had the blood work to confirm the results. She'd had the physical examination and ultrasound today, had been moved to tears over hearing her baby's heartbeat . . . and still it wasn't until she realized that she'd need to fill her home office with a crib and changing table and whatever stuff a baby needed that she finally realized just how much her life was going to change.

No spontaneous trips without planning ahead for childcare or to bring the baby. She'd need sitters and maybe a nanny for the road trips she'd be away. Hell, she'd need a lot more than that—diapers and onesies and . . . baby shampoo.

She didn't even know where to start with that.

Which brands were the best? Would she be able to figure out

how to breastfeed? Also—fuck—was labor going to be as scary and painful and terrifying as they made it look on TV?

Her phone buzzed again, and she grabbed it, knowing it was probably Jason making it clear that he was serious and didn't want anything to do with the baby he'd played sperm donor to, but not caring.

Because she'd rather deal with an asshole than all the scary voices in her head.

Like the ones that were calling her insane for keeping the baby, telling her that she didn't know anything about kids, except how to help them learn to skate and stick-handle, and she didn't think that would be a particularly helpful skill when it came to figuring out how to keep a newborn alive or changing a poopy diaper or figuring out how in the fuck she was going to get some sleep.

She needed to talk to—

Her cell vibrated in her palm and she blinked away the voices, glancing down at the message previewed on the screen.

It was from an unknown number.

It was from . . . Coop.

Or at least, she assumed it was since the message said,

I get why you need to create distance between us. I didn't like the words you used in the process, but I get it. I shouldn't have pushed. I also need you to know I would never do anything to fuck with your career.

Calle yanked her hair back into a ponytail, wrenching all of the pieces into a tight grip that meant no stray hairs would escape.

She didn't need to be quite so aggressive with her locks any longer, it didn't matter if a piece got in her eyes, wouldn't be risking fucking up a play by her field of vision being compromised. But she'd wrestled with her hair for so many years that she couldn't stand the smallest piece tickling her forehead or her cheek.

And . . . none of those random thoughts had a single thing to do with the fact that she now had Coop's number, that he'd sent her a text. A very reasonable and professional text if one ignored the f-bomb stuck near the end of it.

Although, hockey.

So really, the word *fuck* wasn't exactly out of place.

Her phone vibrated once more and as she processed the words Coop had written, her pulse picked up and her guilt from earlier burned even brighter.

God, she was an asshole.

Also, if your brain is taking you down a path that is making the nerves ramp and you question yourself, just know that you're the strongest woman I've ever met. You've got this. The team has your back.

"Fuck," she muttered, setting her phone down and thumping her head onto the back of the couch.

The man was too smart for his own good.

And she had yelled at him.

How was that for professional?

She sat up, grabbed her phone, and began to type out a reply. But then she remembered his face, the anger mixed with hurt. *She'd* done that. She'd hurt him when he'd been lovely and kind and a good man. All because her life was a dumpster fire and she didn't know what the fuck she was doing and—

Her cell dropped back to the cushion.

Her fingers rose and fixed an imaginary stray hair, tightened the tie around her ponytail.

Her lids slid closed.

No. No reply. Nothing but cool, calm, professional distance.

Because she needed to keep that dumpster fire far, *far* away from anyone else, but she most especially needed to keep her dumpster fire, soon to be doctor and lawyer and *diaper*-filled life far, *far* away from Coop.

———

Her intention to stay far, far away from Coop lasted less than twenty-four hours.

Which was to say, he was the lucky soul who walked into the Gold Mine and happened to see her losing her early dinner into a garbage can.

So much for her nausea being manageable.

She'd turned her head when she heard the beep from the lock disengaging, trying to stop puking long enough to pull her shit together and hightail it to her office. But the moment she straightened, the storm in her stomach that had been settling roared to life, and she lost some of the oatmeal she had for breakfast, too.

Her eyes had processed that it was Coop coming through—because *of course* it was Coop—but then she'd been lost in misery and trying not to process what was coming out of her mouth in order to hit the black garbage bag in front of her.

When she eventually stopped, cool fingers lifted her ponytail from the back of her neck, and something damp and cold was draped over the sweaty skin there.

"Okay?" Coop murmured, his expression careful.

She nodded, swallowed, and then immediately wished she hadn't because the aftertaste was . . . she shuddered. "Sorry."

"Nothing to be sorry about," he said softly and handed her a bottle of water he'd grabbed from somewhere. "You good?"

She straightened slowly, used the wet paper towel Coop had placed on her neck to wipe her mouth, then dropped it into the garbage can, stepping away and wanting to forget the entire experience. "Five minutes ago, I would have said, I'm great," she said and took a sip of water. "Now? I'm . . . forever traumatized by industrial trash cans, I think."

His lips quirked. "Morning sickness has turned into evening sickness?"

Calle sighed. "Apparently."

"That sucks."

Silence then she straightened her shoulders, took another cautious drink. Her stomach felt better now, actually. Almost as though she hadn't been sick at all.

If only that were true.

"Thank you," she murmured. She bit her lip, wanting to apologize for last night. "Coop. I'm—"

He took a step back. "I'm going to go get ready."

She nodded. "Right."

Apologize. Just tell him you're sorry you were a dick and apologize and put this all behind you—

"Coop. I'm so—"

The wave of nausea swelled up so quickly that she barely spun around in time. And then she was puking, round two.

"Here." Coop took the bottle from her hand, rested his palm on her nape—

The outside door opened, voices filtering in.

The hand on her neck disappeared.

"Calle!" Brit exclaimed. "Are you okay?"

She nodded as much as she could, given her current situation. But even as she struggled to reassure Brit then Stefan, who came in behind his wife, she felt Coop move away. Some sixth sense told her he was leaving, moving down the hall, and melting out of sight. And when she managed to stop throwing up—or more likely, she ran out of things in her stomach to expel—Calle turned her head.

Yup. He was gone.

"I've been better," she told Brit. Stefan stepped away for a moment, slipping into the workout room that was just a couple of doors down and reemerging with a small white towel and a bottled sports drink.

"Thanks," she said, accepting the items. "But go on. I'm fine. I think I got it all out."

"Dinner didn't sit well?" Stefan asked.

Yeah, that *and* the baby in her uterus had decided to tap dance on her stomach. "Not so much. Thanks for these." She waved a hand in the direction of the locker room. "Go. Don't let me mess up your routine."

"Sure you're good?" Brit asked.

"Totally fine."

Stefan studied her face, concern dancing across his blue eyes, and Calle felt a pulse of humor. These guys. This *girl*. Hell, it was these players. They were eagle-eyed, didn't miss a beat or a change. And . . . they cared. They'd built a family and wanted to keep it whole and healthy.

"I promise I'm fine."

A pair of blond brows joined the concerned blue eyes.

And that was enough of that.

Calle sighed. "Remember who does the practice plans? Maybe I need to go old school, like I used to with my kids? Throw in a few ladder drills?"

Ladder drills consisted of skating back and forth between every line from one end of the ice to the other. They were awful and basic and . . . these guys definitely didn't need their on-ice conditioning to be conducted with old childhood drills.

But it was still fun to threaten the team with them.

Case in point, Stefan shuddered.

"Why don't you throw in some circles, too?" he muttered.

Calle's lips tipped up. "I can do that." A beat. "I'll tell the team it was your special request."

"You're evil again," Brit said. "Which means, you're back!" She did jazz hands for a moment before trying and failing to smother a smile. "Also, Stefan loves ladder drills."

Stefan wrapped an arm around Brit's shoulders. "Not cool." To Calle, he said, "See you in a bit."

"He's getting old," Brit stage whispered as Stefan led her away down the hall. "Ladder drills will help him with his conditioning—"

The teasing was cut off with a kiss as he tugged her into the changing room.

That kiss was cut off by catcalls.

Or at least Calle assumed it ended when the voices from the other players reached her ears in the hallway, teasing and shouted one-liners running rampant. But no one could ever know with Brit and Stefan—they'd been together long enough to not be too worried about their audience.

Hence, the reason the most famous picture of the two of them was after they'd won the Cup, helmets tossed to the ice, arms wrapped tight around one another, lips pressed together.

The door finished its slow slide closed, and the noise disappeared.

Calle pushed the longing away—missing being a player on a team like this, missing playing the game itself, longing that things had turned out differently, longing . . . to have someone in her life like Stefan.

And knowing it wouldn't happen.

Her life didn't have happily-ever-afters.

It had a hardened heart and was filled to the brim with putting her head down and hustling, of making the best of and finding her happy with whatever shitty hand had been dealt her.

Stifling a sigh, she picked up the bottle of water Coop had left, carrying it along with the towel and sports drink down the hall to her office.

She'd set it all on her desk and sat down before she saw what was on the surface.

A package of saltine crackers and a ginger ale.

Coop.

Unbidden, a sliver of affection for the wonderful, pushy, quietly intervening man wove its way through the hardened exterior of her heart.

And Calle didn't know whether to be terrified or hopeful.

Terrified.

She was going with terrified.

Seven

Coop

He left the water running, steam filling the shower room, knowing that someone else would be right in behind him to use the hot water.

There was no shortage of stinky hockey players post-game who needed to shower.

Probably not the best move to leave it on when living in drought-ridden California, but sometimes old habits were hard to break, and not wanting to make his teammates wait forever for the water to heat—something that definitely took less time in an NHL team's locker room than what used to pass as showers in the rinks he'd played at growing up—was one of those old habits he'd never grown out of.

And considering the rest of the team did the same, he supposed he wasn't the only one.

Old dogs. New tricks.

Also, when had he become an old dog?

He wasn't by any means, he supposed. At twenty-seven, he was smack dab in the middle of the guys' ages. Some—Stefan,

Mike, and Blane—were considering retirement . . . or at least what their lives would look like once their contracts were up.

In their early to mid-thirties, *they* were the old dogs, they were the ones who were at the ends of their careers. A brutal fact, yes, but professional sports tended toward a young man's game and they'd won the Cup, had great seasons, been part of a great team. Hockey, especially when they were getting paid to play, and needed to treat it like the job it was, didn't get much better than that.

Coop knew.

He'd been on a few rosters that had almost managed to suck the soul out of him.

Players who were prima donnas. Coaches who thought they could only get the best out of their teams by screaming and throwing shit and punishments.

Look, sometimes a team needed their asses chewed between periods or after a game, but they didn't *always* need it, and it certainly took away any of the shock and fired-up response they might pull from the roster if the team knew they would be facing their coach's temper tantrum any time they were in the locker room.

So, it was lucky that Coop had ended up here.

With the Gold.

With Bernard and Calle and the rest of the coaching staff. They might hold them to a high standard, but they held themselves to the same expectations and because of it, the players knew if they fucked up or had a bad game or hell, if the hockey gods didn't happen to be speaking that night, that their backs were still covered.

They might get extra tape or pulled into an office for a chat, but that Coop got, *that* made for better players.

That made for a family.

He walked out of the locker room, snagged a towel from the rack just outside the doorway, and saw that Calle was sitting next to Kevin, now dressed in his suit, both their eyes on the tablet in front of them.

Coop shook out the towel, started to wrap it around his hips.

But then Kevin nodded and Calle stood, closing the cover on the tablet, her gaze leaving Kevin and heading in his direction. And so, maybe he took a little bit longer than normal wrapping the cotton around his hips, especially when her eyes hit his and froze before darting down, and those lush pink lips parted slightly.

He slowly tucked one end of the towel into the other and strode through the changing room to his stall.

Calle's head jerked away, feet retreating toward the door.

"Calle?" Kevin called.

Hesitantly, she spun back around. "Yeah?"

"Can you show Coop that same play?" he asked. "I think it'll help for the next game."

Coop froze, searching his teammate's expression for a moment before relaxing.

Kevin's was both a completely innocent suggestion, as well as a totally professional one, seeing as they'd had a home and home series against the Ducks (the Ducks played at the Gold Mine for a game and then they went down to Anaheim for the next). Plus, Kevin wasn't known for his poker face. His heart lived on his sleeve, and that was part of why he'd been able to snag the beautiful, capable Rebecca. If he was matchmaking, Coop would know it, and that was because his friend was known for out-stubborning Rebecca into giving him a chance.

And then out-stubborning her to stay around.

Calle crossed over to them, and her expression would have given PR-Rebecca a run for her money in the stubborn department.

Or maybe it was determined.

Determined to prove to him—or herself—that nothing had changed between them and that she was fully capable of that.

Well, he knew *that*. The *that* being her ability to be fully capable of doing her job. The other *that*—the nothing had changed one—wasn't so easy to prove. Something had changed, had linked them together, and there was a reason chains weren't easy to break. Links were strong, links tied, links—

Calle shoved the tablet under his nose, thankfully cutting off his internal waxing poetic about links and chains.

"Watch this," she said and hit play.

Coop watching himself on the television feed was still a trip, even after almost seven full seasons in the league. But there he was. He'd obtained his dream, was wearing the jersey of a professional team, and on TV.

Craziness.

But then his mind shifted out of the clouds and down to the screen. He watched the figure move, began to process what the teams were doing, what *he* had done, and he glanced up at Calle, mouth curved. "So, that's what we've been working on, huh?"

Her expression turned playful. "If by *working on* you mean by doing the exact opposite of what we've been practicing, then yes."

"Damn." He grinned.

Her eyes danced before growing earnest as she explained another place they could improve. "And see this here . . ."

His smile faded as she talked, not liking that he hadn't been able to do what she asked, that the things they'd worked on in practice hadn't translated into the game. All that work for absolutely nothing. All of *Calle's* work for nothing. Fuck. What was the point of practicing if he couldn't bring it out in the games?

"Fuck," Blue muttered with a scowl. He'd walked over, was watching alongside Coop. Then he pointed to the screen. "There." Calle paused the video. "It's all going as planned, and then I turn the wrong way—"

"And I slide up too high," Coop interrupted.

"And then an odd-man rush the other way," Calle said.

"I don't like odd-man rushes," Kevin muttered. "Fucking hate back-checking."

Damn. Coop remembered the play now. The puck had

popped out of the zone and the Duck's center had grabbed it, hauling ass along with two of his teammates as they headed toward Brit in goal. Only Stefan had been back playing defense since Mike had overcommitted and ventured too low, and then with him and Blue bungling the offense in one heartbeat and Kevin in too deep, the play's tide had turned.

Three on one was never good odds.

But three on one in professional hockey was even worse.

Even with Brit in net and Stefan, one of the best defensemen, back, the Ducks had still scored. Brit having made the first save but not having been able to make the second.

She'd been pissed about that, about letting the Ducks get the go-ahead goal, but the team didn't blame her, and Coop most certainly didn't. At any given time, the puck had to get through the five of them on the ice before it got to Brit in net, and at that time, three out of the five of them had screwed the pooch, making her odds even worse.

She couldn't make the crazy, game-saving, stand-on-her-head stop every single time.

Even though she expected herself to.

Coop had overheard her talking to Frankie after the game, already planning an extra practice session to improve "her pathetic glove hand" the next game.

Perfectionist.

One of the best goalies he'd ever had the privilege of playing with.

Calle tapped the tablet's screen, and he watched the play unfold, watched the goal, and knew Brit wasn't the only one who needed an extra practice session. He'd set something up, work on plugging that hole until he was perfect.

"I don't expect you guys to be perfect," Calle said, directly contradicting his thoughts. "This is a new system, and there will be hiccups and setbacks as we move forward with it. But the more time and practice and game play with it, the less often we'll see these errors. It's just a matter of muscle memory."

He nodded, meeting Blue's then Kevin's eyes over her shoulder. He knew his line mates were on the same page. More practice. More reps. Fewer imperfections. Fewer outright fuck-ups.

"Thanks, Coach."

Calle may not expect perfection from them, but *he* did. And so, fine, maybe that wasn't reasonable, and maybe Brit wasn't the only obsessive perfectionist in the locker room. So, what if she had plenty of company? They all had to have some perfectionist in them, otherwise they wouldn't have gotten as far as they had.

She nodded and stood. "I'll see you all on the bus."

Coop nodded, wanting to ask if the crackers and ginger ale had helped settle her stomach but knowing that he should just leave it alone. For all he knew, she'd tossed them in the trash and had gone about her game prep. So, instead of asking her about her nausea and the snack, he started to get dressed. By the time he grabbed his own snack and retrieved his shit from his car, there wouldn't be much time before he had to head to the airport with the guys.

The team tended to fly out right away after games, giving them as much time as possible to get to their destination and allowing for issues with delays or flight cancelations.

The second wasn't so common, as the team had their own plane, but sometimes the weather—especially in fog-prone San Francisco—made it tricky to fly out.

So, a bus to the airport then a plane down to Anaheim . . . then a bus to the hotel.

Then tomorrow a bus to the rink.

Then a bus back to the airport.

Pro at hockey. Pro at bus travel.

Not that the buses the team had were anything like those he'd grown up using. These were luxurious with comfortable seats, plenty of legroom, and they even had seat belts.

Cue sarcasm.

But growing up in Atlanta didn't exactly bring the word luxury to mind, or at least not his neighborhood. He'd grown up in a strictly middle-class area, and the hockey opportunities weren't particularly plentiful, but he'd had natural talent and his parents had made it work.

That had meant a lot of driving for them when he'd made a decent travel team, and plenty of him navigating the local transit systems with his huge equipment bag and sticks. Eventually, it had meant allowing him to move in with a family in Michigan so he could take advantage of the better hockey there and could grow as a player. They'd made trips up to watch him play, had scrimped and saved to buy him new skates when his feet grew out of them twice in one season, and they'd never failed to find a way to help him realize his dreams.

Luckily, he'd been able to pay some of that back.

He'd bought them a house last year, had paid off both of their cars—and the only reason he hadn't bought them new ones was because they'd thrown such a conniption about the house that he'd refrained.

He'd still paid for them to take a two-week vacation to an all-inclusive in Jamaica.

They'd come back from fourteen days of sand and surf and free alcohol much more sanguine about the house.

Still wouldn't let him buy them new cars, though.

Grinning, Coop shoved his feet into his shoes and tossed his suit jacket over one arm then gathered up his wallet, cell, and bag. He'd run to his car and get everything sorted. But as he moved to the door, he noticed that Calle hadn't made it very far. She was talking to Brit near the exit and . . . she was looking noticeably pale.

And sweaty.

She swallowed hard, glanced toward the door, and he watched her spine stiffen, her jaw clench, and her shoulders come up.

Did Brit not see that she was dying to get out of the room?

Max came in then, still wearing his post-game workout gear, and Coop watched him stop by Calle and start jabbering.

And all the while, Calle got paler.

He closed the distance between them, saw she'd taken on an almost gray cast and her forehead was beaded with sweat. Max and Brit seemed oblivious. Fuck. How was he the only one who noticed that Calle was breathing through her mouth and inching toward the door?

There were only two feet between them when Max lifted his arm, pointing over Brit's shoulder.

Calle gagged.

Which both Brit and Max missed, because they were looking in the direction he'd pointed, but which Coop definitely *didn't* miss because he was focused on Calle.

"See?" Max was saying, and when Coop got a whiff of the funk that was wafting from beneath Max's armpit, he almost gagged himself.

Fuck, that was awful.

He nudged Max away—okay, he shoved Max—but the six-foot-two-hundred-pound-plus athlete could take it without a backward step. "Hit the showers, dude," he snapped. "You're stinking up the place."

Max smirked. "Don't tell me you like the locker room as clean as you like your car."

Brit snorted.

"It was one time," Coop said, interjecting himself into the conversation and giving Calle a light nudge toward the hall, trying to encourage her to take the chance at escape while she had it.

She understood the push and stepped out of the circle of conversation, slipping quietly into the hall as Max continued teasing him about his obsessively clean car.

Brit joined in then turned the razzing to Max and his collection of toys.

Which then turned to Brit and her taste in music, several of the guys joining in and lamenting about how awful it was when she got to choose the playlist in the locker room.

"You guys know you love Lizzo," Brit said as Stefan came up behind her and slipped his arm around her waist. She turned into the embrace. "You know the guys *love* Lizzo. And Britney. And Gaga. *And* the Backstreet Boys."

Coop shuddered—though he couldn't say he hated when *Juice* came on. That shit was catchy.

Stefan, good husband that he was, nodded and pressed a kiss to her cheek.

Which then turned the teasing Stefan's way, the guys dissecting the many ways he showed Brit way too much PDA in varying degrees of grossness.

And that was Coop's cue to get the fuck out.

He melted into the hallway, intending to go out to the parking lot, but as he walked past the row of offices, he heard it.

It being . . . the sound of vomiting.

One guess whose office it was coming from.

EIGHT

CALLE

The knock at the door as she was quietly trying to lose her cookies was not welcome.

Nor was said door cracking open and the soft voice saying, "It's me."

Because, of course, Coop was there.

She straightened from the trash can she had been losing Coop's crackers and ginger ale into—courtesy of Max and Brit's combined post-game funk—and smiled at the man infiltrating her space again.

"Hey, Coach," he said, eyes going behind him and then forward again. "I was hoping you could show me—"

He slipped through the door and shut it behind him.

"Are you okay?" he asked without preamble once it clicked closed.

She wiped her mouth with the back of her hand. "What do you think?"

"I *think* you look like a corpse."

Since that was an adequate description of how she was feeling, Calle didn't get offended. Instead, stomach settling, she set down the trash can and reached for the top drawer of her desk. If puking through the day was going to become a habit, she'd need to start keeping a toothbrush or mouthwash on hand. For now, she thought she had a pack of gum somewhere mixed in the clutter.

"Well, I've felt better," she muttered, knocking aside stacks of Post-Its, dislodging carefully stowed pens and pencils—

"What are you looking for?"

Not finding the gum, she sighed and shut the drawer. "My mouth feels like a dumpster," she said. She had her toothbrush packed away. She would get it out, sneak into the bathroom to brush her teeth, and that would make everything better.

See? Good plan.

"Here."

Coop's hand appeared in her line of sight.

Not as close as Max's had been, the big defensemen managed to create a funk that even their equipment manager's vast skills at keeping the hockey smell at bay couldn't manage. Still, Coop was close enough that she caught a whiff of his scent, of something spicy and masculine that definitely didn't make her feel nauseated.

Hell, it was about as far away from nauseated as she could get.

Heat coiled in her belly, seeping out to fill her limbs, to snake down between her thighs, to make her knees—both damaged and whole—wobble just the tiniest bit.

Her fingers trembled when she reached for the pack of mints he'd held out. "Thanks," she murmured.

"Any time."

She took one, popped it into her mouth, and started to hand the container back.

He waved her away. "Keep them."

"Thanks," she said again and picked up her water bottle, taking a long sip to clear away the final unpleasant taste of being sick.

The edges of her favorite smile in the history of all smiles appeared, curving his mouth up, making his eyes sparkle with amusement. The effect was as physical as getting nailed into the boards during a battle.

Breath-stealing and a punch to the gut at the same time.

"I figure your need is greater than mine," he teased.

Her own lips curved up. "I think I spoke too soon about the nausea thing to Dr. Holdings."

"Unfortunately, I think you're right." He opened his mouth then just as quickly closed it again.

"What?" she asked.

"It's not my place," he said. "Hope the mints help." He reached for the doorknob. "See you on the—"

His words cut off.

Probably because she'd touched his back.

Probably because she *had* touched his back, intending to tell him . . . something that *poofed* away like so much smoke when her brain processed the spike of heat that coursed through the thin cotton of his button-down. He was scorching hot, and at the contact, a spark lit through her fingers, almost burning in its intensity and ramping up the yearning she'd felt over the last two seasons.

She wanted to jump into that fire, to get burned to ash, to—

Coop slowly turned around, and his dark eyes were molten, scalding her, stealing her breath, causing moisture to pool between her thighs.

She swallowed hard, almost choking on the mint.

His hand came up, cupped her cheek. "Careful," he murmured.

How in the hell could she be careful when he made her feel like this? How in the hell could she step back when all she wanted to do was move forward?

There was a reason she'd slept with Jason almost three months before, and that was because she was lonely and empty and . . . had been craving Coop with an increasingly frightening need. But that need wasn't going away like she'd hoped, and spending all this extra time with him wasn't helping.

Her muscles ached from resisting the urge to launch herself into his arms.

She needed—

His thumb, lightly calloused like her own, drifted along her cheek, and then his palm drifted down, sliding along her jaw, her throat, her arm, slipping around behind her back and pulling her flush against his front.

Fuck, that was good.

Her breasts brushed the hard lines of his chest, his stomach, and him being just a few inches taller than her meant that their mouths lined up perfectly.

They were close enough that she could feel his breath against her lips, his scent was flooding her senses, but instead of making her nauseated, she felt intoxicated. "You're like catnip," she murmured, rubbing her face against his chest.

Coop froze, and she realized what she'd said.

How inane it must have sounded.

She tried to back up, to pull out of his hold, but his arms just tightened, holding her against him. Hell, she had to be honest. She wasn't trying very hard to get away, inane statements or not. She felt too good being held in his arms.

Still, she didn't want to sound like an idiot.

"I—I meant—I'm just tired—" A shake of her head. "Ignore me. Apparently, all this throwing up has made it so I can't speak in normal sentences—"

Her excuses cut off because Coop dropped his head, inhaling deeply. "Well, baby," he murmured, hot breath ruffling her hair, making a shiver skate down her spine, "if I'm your catnip, then know I've been fantasizing about bottling the scent of you for months. It makes my mouth water and my cock get hard every time I smell it."

It wasn't until her lungs burned and her head began to spin that she realized she'd sucked in a breath and held it. Her lips parted, the long-held air shuddered out and . . . she melted against Coop's chest.

Even though it was probably the stupidest thing she'd ever done.

Even though she should back up and let him leave.

Even though this had disaster written all over it.

"Calle?"

She'd dropped her forehead against his pecs again, had been inhaling his scent again, letting it wash over her and heat her from the inside out. "Hmm?"

"I'm going to kiss you now."

Her head shot up.

Her lungs stopped working.

Her brain screamed no . . . okay, lie, it screamed yes.

Her pussy demanded she drop her pants and bend over the desk so he could take her from behind.

Her tongue . . . well, *that* fucker started a mutiny by practically shouting, right in Coop's face, "No!"

Her body joined in, lurching from the circle of his arms.

Her eyes caught the flash of hurt sliding across his face.

Her—

"I—"

He shook his head. "No explanation needed," he said darkly. "I'm reading you loud and clear—"

"No!" Another almost shout. Another ridiculous outburst. And look, she got it. She was acting like an insane person, melting in his hold one second, screaming at him the next. "I *want* to kiss you," she said, probably stupidly, certainly imprudently given her job and the current state of her life. "I've been dreaming about what you'd taste like for months and . . ."

His eyes softened. "Your job."

"Yes." A sigh. "No. *Yes.* I don't know." She reached up to tug at her ponytail then remembered she'd taken it down and carefully brushed it before the game, wanting, vainly, to look her best on camera.

"Sweetheart, I get it," he said. "I'll just go so you don't have to—"

Sweetheart. Her heart pulsed. *God,* what would it be like if she lived in a reality where she could be with him, where she could hear him calling her baby and sweetheart for the rest of her days? She wanted that reality so badly, even as she knew it would never happen. Because, aside from the conflict their jobs brought, no man in his right mind would want to be with a newly pregnant woman who was carrying another man's baby—let alone one as beautiful as Coop, who was a talented athlete and hotter even than her favorite celebrity to crush on, Idris Elba.

And yet, she didn't want Coop to think she didn't want him. The thought of hurting the lovely, sweet, wonderful man she'd come to know over the last two years was untenable.

Which was when her tongue went on another mutiny.

"I-don't-want-you-to-kiss-me-because-I-just-puked."

His brows lifted. "What was that?"

Oh God. She spun around, hands coming up to cover her face. She couldn't say it again. She couldn't—

"I don't want you to kiss me because I just puked," she said softly, dropping her hands but hanging her head. "I'm gross and probably taste horrible, and I can't have your mouth on mine or your tongue—" A short breath. "I want to, but—"

Just. Stop. Talking.

Silence.

Then the *click* of the door opening and closing.

A slice of hurt cut through her. Well, she'd done a good job of running him off by being honest. She should have just tried that from the beginning, pushing him away by telling him the truth and revealing—

"*Oof.*"

She was spun around, her front plastered to Coop's front, belatedly realizing that the click she'd heard was the lock engaging, not the door opening and closing.

"Why in the fuck do you think that I would give a shit about you being sick?" he growled, mouths millimeters apart, hot breath on her lips.

"Because I might taste—"

"You had a fucking mint," he snapped. "You drank water."

"I—" She *had* done that.

"Does your mouth taste bad to you?"

Mutely, she shook her head.

"So, why would I think that it would?"

Her chin came up, muteness faded. "People have bad breath all the time without realizing it."

He inhaled. "You smell like mint and roses and sugar. You smell good enough to lick."

Mute came back.

"I've smelled Max, sweetheart. I've spent my life around gross hockey players who seem to think it's their job to spit and snot everywhere. Why in the would you think that a beautiful woman who smells like peppermint and roses would turn me off?"

"You're insane. Any other man would think—"

"I'm *not* any other man."

Her heart skipped a beat, a wave of heat washed over her from head to toe. No. No, he wasn't like any other man she'd ever met.

Probably, she should have focused or stepped back or made up an excuse to get him to leave.

But she didn't.

Because she wanted him to kiss her, more than she'd ever wanted anything else.

And that was the last rational thought she had.

"I'm going to kiss you now," he murmured and paused, probably waiting for another tongue mutiny and when it didn't come, his eyes went hot, his grip on her tightened, and she found herself pressed even more firmly against him.

His mouth dropped, and he closed the last few millimeters between their lips.

NINE

COOP

Honey.

Calle tasted like honey—sweet and earthy albeit with a hint of mint. But he had the barest moment to think of that before her lips parted and heat exploded through his body. He swept his tongue into her mouth, coaxing hers to dance with his.

Frankly, it didn't take much coaxing.

Her hands gripped his shoulders tightly, and she pulled him toward her. Fuck, just the feel of her breasts plastered against his chest had him going hard. He slid his hand down her back to her ass, tugged her closer, and she jumped into his arms, legs going around his waist, mouth pressing more firmly against his and sending him from hard to granite.

All the while, they kissed like the world was ending or as though they were each other's favorite drug and they were desperate to get their next fix.

Then her hips tilted, and Coop stopped thinking.

Instead, he felt.

The soft globes of her ass in his hands. The smell of her filling his nose. The heat of her pussy grinding against his cock.

Fuck, he needed to be naked.

Fuck, he needed *her* to be naked.

Her head jerked back, and she sucked in air, chest rising and falling in rapid succession. He let his mouth drop to her jaw, nipping the soft, honey-sweet skin there, dragging his tongue down her throat, tracing it along the collar of her almost-prudish dress shirt. She always wore them to the games, and he'd lost count of the number of times he'd imagined unbuttoning the column of white circular fastenings, of spreading the boring cotton wide and getting his mouth on all of that pale, silky skin.

Her legs tightened and he took a step forward, setting her on the edge of her desk, before bending further and opening the top button with a flick of his fingers.

She moaned, hands moving toward his hair, winding tight.

He dropped his head.

Just a quick taste.

His mouth hit her throat, and he groaned, the scent of her stronger here and more intoxicating than the catnip she'd been mentioning earlier. He kissed her there, laved his tongue gently over the slight indention, but he couldn't reach much more than a small triangle of skin.

Okay, just one more button.

He reached up to open it, but then Calle tugged his head back up and slanted her mouth across his.

Fuck, the woman could kiss.

Not shy, not hesitant. Just lips and tongue and teeth . . . and a whole lot of enthusiasm. Coop's head spun and his cock was aching, especially when her thighs tightened around his waist and he got to feel the heat of her pussy grinding against him again.

Thanking the universe for small miracles—namely that the dress pants they both wore were thin and didn't dim much of the sensation—he ran his hand back up to the buttons, flicking one . . . then two . . . then fuck it all, *three* open.

They both groaned when he cupped her breast over her bra.

But he wanted skin. He *needed* skin.

He slipped his hand under her shirt and was rewarded with silk, with a breast that fit perfectly in the palm of his hand, its pebbled nipple making him shift his grip and lightly pinch it between thumb and forefinger.

"Coop!" she gasped, arching into his hold.

He slanted his lips against hers again, swallowing her moans as he continued to tease her nipple, to massage her breast. His pulse thundered in his veins. His head spun. He wasn't getting enough air and yet he couldn't stop kissing her, couldn't find the strength to break away from the fucking goddess in front of him.

And she seemed to feel the same.

She tugged his head back when he broke away to suck in a breath, her thighs so tight around him he was lucky to still have feeling in his lower extremities, let alone blood flow to his dick, arching up to offer her breast to his hand, pressing her pussy more firmly against him.

He kissed her, *kept* kissing her.

And now he was ten seconds away from fucking her on her desk.

One more button.

Another.

Reaching behind to flick open her bra.

Releasing her mouth, bending to take one nipple then the other into his mouth, drawing deeply. He undid the last button—this one being the one on her pants—and slipped his hand beneath the waistband, beneath the scrap of material underneath, into the damp folds between her thighs.

She spread her legs as much as she was able.

But it was enough.

His fingers dipped down and found—

Hot. Wet.

For him.

"Fuck, Coop," she groaned, hips jerking. He circled the hard bundle of nerves at the apex of her thighs, finding a rhythm that quickly had her writhing on her desk, head thrown back, brown hair spread out like a cape behind her. "More," she gasped. "Just a little harder on my clit. I'm so close . . . *Yes*. I'm going to—"

He heard the knock before she did.

Thankfully, he managed to reach up and cover her mouth with his palm, to stifle the groan as she came against his hand, her nipple against his tongue, her pussy soaking wet against his fingers.

So. Fucking. Beautiful.

She slumped back, face completely relaxed, cheeks flushed, eyes sliding closed for one glorious moment.

Then the knock came again.

And those eyes flashed open.

Horror washed over her face. Chased by panic. Followed again by horror.

Coop was two steps ahead of her. Well, what he was feeling definitely wasn't horror or panic, but he knew that being discovered splayed out half-naked on her desk wasn't what Calle would want . . . even if he'd just given her what seemed to be a long-overdue orgasm.

Hence, the two steps.

He'd slipped his hand free, buttoned her slacks, and was working on her shirt when she finally processed what was happening.

She sat up, shoved him away, fingers frantic on the buttons, making such a mess of the discs that he knocked her hands away and did them up himself. That she let him, told him almost as much as her pale face and wild eyes did.

He'd miscalculated.

He shouldn't have kissed her.

He *certainly* shouldn't have undone the buttons.

Fuck.

But he didn't have the ability to go back in time. He could only move forward, so Coop nudged her around to the back of the desk, opened the tablet, and then reached into his pocket to pull out his earbuds.

He'd just handed one to her and pulled up the video she showed him earlier when he heard the click of the lock disengaging just before Bernard poked his head in.

Coach looked surprised to see them, his eyes tracking from the earbuds in Coop and Calle's hands to the iPad on the desk.

Silence.

"Door was locked," he said, gruffly.

"What?" Calle asked, and it was bewildered . . . no doubt from the orgasm and near desk-fucking, but luckily it also fit this situation.

"Coach was just showing me some tape," Coop interjected.

Bernard's eyes went down and up again. "Didn't hear the knock?"

"No, sorry," Coop said. "Had the earbuds in."

"Ah."

Another long searching look. "The bus is scheduled to leave in ten."

Coop stood, leaving the earbud on Calle's desk and hoping she'd grab them both and find a way to get them back to him because otherwise it would be a long-ass flight with all of Max's nattering about the latest—and best in the history of all bests—fantasy show on television.

But he thought it would be even weirder to ask for it back from Calle while Bernard was still there, and he'd lied enough.

"I'd better hurry and go grab my stuff," he announced to no one in particular.

His eyes caught Calle's just before he left, and the look in them cemented the sinking sensation in his gut. He might have explained the situation, might have managed to not make Bernard suspicious—or minimally so, anyway—but she was terrified and already retreating.

Already pulling back and out of grasp.

Just like before.

Fuck.

Coop had really screwed the pooch on this one.

———

"Hi, Mom," he said, hugging her and tugging her down the hall, carefully skirting the locker room where a bunch of naked dudes —and at least until a few minutes ago, one naked dudette—

And had he really just said *dudette*?

Because seriously, California had corrupted him. No self-respecting Georgian said dude, let alone the female equivalent. Also, side note to ask one of the native Californians on staff, was dude a gender-neutral term? It seemed like it should be and—

His mother squeezed his arm, thankfully tugging him out of the mental rabbit hole he'd wandered down. "Is that *Brit Plantain?*" she asked, wonder in her words.

"Yeah, Mom," he said, leading her over to his teammate.

"She's my favorite player," his mom whispered.

"I know," he whispered back, not even giving her his usual shtick about his rights as her son to be in that role. He glanced over his shoulder, saw his dad was smiling, already realizing what Coop had done.

His mom had been devastated the last time his parents had visited the team—bringing enough delicious Southern food to feed an army, thankfully on a cheat day from Nutritionist Rebecca's diet plan—only to miss Brit. The goalie had been visiting a local school that day and hadn't been to the arena, and then the timing for a post-game meet-up hadn't worked because of his parents' return flight.

When Coop had heard his parents were going to catch his game here in Anaheim before heading to San Diego to visit his sister, he knew he'd remedy that.

His mom's feet started to drag when she recognized the direction he was taking her. "Coop, *stop*. I can't meet her now. My hair"—she reached up and patted her perfectly coiffed locks—

"my shirt"—a sharp shake of her head. "No. She wouldn't care about that." Wide eyes swiveled to Coop's. "What if I mess up her post-game routine and—"

Brit was already chatting with Mandy while doing her usual stretching routine, one that involved a wall and a series of exercises to keep her bum shoulder intact. She also never shied away from a chat with a fan, and he'd already cleared this meet-up with her.

She knew he was bringing his mom over.

After more than a few seasons in the league, she was also really good at reading social situations.

And she used her powers for good.

For the most part.

Today, thankfully, her gaze drifted over and dipped, probably taking in his mom's attempts to halt his forward progress. She turned back to Mandy, said something, and then pushed off the wall and headed toward them.

His mom froze, and Coop heard her inhale sharply.

Then Brit was there.

"Hey," Coop said. "This is my mom, Doreen."

Brit smiled widely—the same one that had garnered her more than a few endorsements over the years. "You made that delicious mac and cheese!" she exclaimed, reaching out and shaking his mom's hand. "Thankfully, Stefan saved me some before the hoard devoured it all. It's so nice to meet you!"

His mom's mouth opened and closed a few times, but no words came out.

Thankfully, Brit was nonplussed. She tucked her arm into his mom's and turned to face Coop's dad.

"Hi," he said, reaching out to shake her hand. "I'm Daniel. Thanks for saving my son's butt on the breakaway."

Brit's lips twitched. "Technically, it was my hubby's fault that puck slipped out, but I'll take it out of his paycheck later," she said with a wink. "It's nice to meet you, too. Now, Coop tells me your daughter recently moved to San Diego. Have you gone down to visit her already?"

"We're actually driving down tonight," his mom answered, having relaxed enough to actually form words.

Then the conversation was off, Brit and his mom chatting like old friends, discussing the drive and things to do and then Coop's sister and her plans for her new job in California.

"We may have to move out here now that two of our kids have switched coasts," his mom said. "The weather's beautiful and . . ."

They discussed the beaches and how SoCal was lucky enough to have an ocean that was warm enough to not hurt one's feet when they walked the waves—which was Brit's preference and definitely not the case up in the Bay Area. Mandy popped in briefly with a Sharpie—smart, considerate, and sweet were the top three terms to describe their trainer out of the PT suite; in it, she was often called evil, tormenting, and unsympathetic—but either way, she brought the pen and then his mom got her jersey signed by none other than Brit Plantain.

Coop could have sent her a signed one at any point during the last few seasons, but it wouldn't have been the same, and he wouldn't have gotten to see the look on his mom's face.

Joy.

He'd brought her joy.

His dad nodded approvingly then Brit drew him into the conversation as well. He watched his father slip his arm around his mom's waist and draw her into his side, felt a pulse at knowing he didn't have that yet.

That being a partner who fit as perfectly into his life as his parents did into each other's.

And at the rate he was going, it was unlikely he ever would.

Stifling a sigh, he tried to focus back on the conversation, but then he looked up and saw Calle.

One glance was all it took for his heart rate to spike, for a sliver of heat to shoot down his spine, but then she came closer, in an intense conversation with Bernard, the both of them apparently unaware of the collection of Armstrongs jamming the hall. Calle was close enough for Coop to smell the floral scent of her shampoo—or maybe that was just him hallucinating because he'd dreamed about her the night before. Either way, she and Bernard halted, their conversation breaking off.

This is where you talk.

Except, his brain wasn't working. Calle was there and the tips of his fingers burned remembering the wet heat of her, his cock twitched wanting a repeat, and his heart twisted upon seeing the look on her face.

Panic chased by a mask of indifference.

Fucking hell.

He silently sucked in a breath and just as silently, released it. *Enough. Head down. Eyes forward.*

"Hey, Coach. These are my parents," he said. "Daniel and Doreen. Mom, Dad, these are my coaches—Bernard and Calle."

Pleasantries were exchanged, well, pleasantries were exchanged between most of them because Bernard wasn't exactly known for being particularly pleasant. But he was at least on good behavior, and Calle was her usual charming self as they chatted for a few minutes before they said their goodbyes, moving on down the hall and continuing with the serious conversation.

Coop's eyes followed.

He couldn't help it.

Calle was just . . . he'd had a taste of the forbidden and was ruined.

Not to be. Not to be. Not to—

His dad punched his arm. Not lightly either. Frowning, Coop spun back around—okay, so maybe he hadn't realized he'd turned so far from the group or tuned so far out of the conversation when he'd watched her walk away.

"What?" he asked.

His dad studied his face. Then sighed and said quietly, "Careful with that one, son."

"I'm always careful, Dad," Coop said just as quietly. "We work together. I wouldn't jeopardize—"

His dad shook his head. "Not what I meant."

"What *did* you mean?"

He opened his mouth to answer Coop, but then his mom gasped. "Oh no, Brit! I couldn't. I just couldn't possibly accept something so—" He turned his head to see that Brit was giving his mom a stick and a glove, both game-used by the looks of it.

They argued for a few seconds before Brit managed to get his mom to accept the gift, but then, as Coop and Brit had known she would, his mom had given in, tears drifting down her cheeks as she threw her arms around Brit.

"I know I tease Coop about you being my favorite player, but aside from my son, you truly are. I remember watching you in your first NHL game and just being so blown away by how calm and composed you were." She sniffed and pulled back. "And then you led my baby to winning a Cup, and he got his dream." She sniffed again, but this time tears dripped down her cheeks. "Oh, Lord. I'm not normally this much of an emotional mess—"

"Yes, you are," Coop teased.

She glared, but her mouth was curving. "I have been known to cry at dog food commercials."

Brit cocked her head to the side, expression questioning.

"The puppies just look so h-happy—"

His dad tutted, pulling the stick and glove out of his wife's hands and shoving them at Coop, before tugging her against his chest and holding her tight.

She let him, snuggling in, and Coop turned to Brit, who was smiling.

"Dog food commercials?" she asked lightly.

He nodded. "Every time."

She chuckled.

"Thanks for doing that," he said softly. "You made her year."

"She's a riot."

"She's *something*," he agreed.

"I'll have you know," his mom said, tears dried. "I used to be all tough and scary, but then this man"—she poked at her husband—"just relentlessly, pulled all of my tough girl armor away, and now I'm a big softie who cries at dog food commercials."

"I know what that's like," Brit said, expression softening.

Coop's mom smiled. "I'm glad you do, honey." A beat. "Just don't let the guys know, or I'd imagine they'd give you hell for it."

"They could try," Brit said in a sing-song voice, "but then I'd torture them with more pop music in the locker room and all vengeance would be enacted."

Coop snorted.

His mom grinned.

His dad kissed her on the top of her head. "I liked the tough girl," he said, quietly, though Coop still heard. "But I love the cries-at-dog-food woman with all my heart."

His mom murmured something back and then as they often found themselves, Coop's parents, slid into their own world, lost in each other, their love for each other palpable.

Apparently, Brit saw it, too, because she sighed and when he glanced over at her face, it was to see a gentle expression there, her eyes damp with tears.

"Your parents are pretty cool, Coop," she said.

"I know," he said.

"I'm going to go find Stefan," she announced, then spent a few moments saying goodbye before disappearing down the hall.

"I'm glad she found a good man," his mom said as he led them out of the bowels of the arena and walked them to their car. "She deserves to have someone who makes her happy."

He voiced his agreement, but all he could think as they drove away was what about him finding someone who made *him* happy?

Unfortunately, Coop had the feeling that there was only one woman on the planet who could do that.

And he couldn't have her.

His phone buzzed a couple hours later as he rode the team bus to the airport.

It was a message from his dad.

I meant careful because you need to tread carefully. That heart of hers is fragile. Anyone with half a brain can see it.

Couldn't go there. Coop absolutely could *not* go there.

But still . . . the text made him wonder if it might actually be possible.

At least for a moment, because then he tucked all of that longing safely away. *No.* He couldn't do that to Calle.

She needed protection. Not risk.

———

The remainder of the trip was a disaster.

Not because of his parents' visit or that the team had played horribly during the game.

In fact, the hole that Calle had identified had been plugged, and no one had over-committed to the play or missed their coverage. They'd easily trounced the Ducks, and the team was heading home on a high note. Plus, his mom had been beyond thrilled and her time with Brit had gone better than he could have hoped.

His relationship with Calle on the other hand?

Not so much.

And when had he started calling it a relationship?

Probably right about the time he'd seen her eyes tear up when she'd heard her baby's heartbeat. Or maybe when his tongue had been in her mouth, his fingers sliding through the damp folds of her pussy.

He shifted, adjusting the thin material of his slacks and deliberately turned his mind away from the memory of that kiss, of her coming against his fingers all hot and wet before he popped a fucking hard-on while riding in the team's plane. With his luck, Max or Blue would notice, and then the guys wouldn't just be teasing him about the inside of his car, but his teenage-boy-like qualities.

Sighing, he shoved his earbuds in—luckily for him, Calle had dropped them into his lap when she'd walked by his seat on the plane down to Anaheim as she'd headed toward the back where the coaches clustered.

It had made the short flight much more palatable.

Not that he didn't like his teammates, but it was nearly one, and they were once again packed into a plane, knowing that even after they landed, they still had another bus ride back to the rink and their cars before they all drove home. And no matter how luxurious the team's private plane and buses were, traveling was still Coop's least favorite part. He just wanted to be at the arena, and further that, he just wanted to be on the ice, blades strapped to his feet, stick in his hands.

Hockey had always been his happy place.

Thankfully, having it as his career hadn't changed that.

There was absolutely nothing like hearing the crowd chant his name, of feeling that cool, crisp air hit his skin as he made his way onto the rink, of the electric sensation when he scored a goal or got to celebrate a teammate's.

It was hockey. It was his lifeblood.

It was everything.

A whiff of flowers hit his nose, and Coop's eyes flew up. He saw that Calle was moving past his seat, walking down the aisle toward the rear of the plane.

Her eyes, those pretty milk chocolate depths, were averted, and he knew in his gut that it was deliberate. It was late, the second travel night in as many days. Everyone was tired and ready to get back home, to have a full two days off, including him.

But Calle had always sent a smile in his direction when their paths crossed, tired or not.

That ten minutes in her office had been the single best sexual experience of his life, even though he hadn't come, even though it had been far too short, even though it had been interrupted.

Because she was incredible.

He'd thought so for a long time, even before she'd come to the Gold, when he'd watched the women win gold, when he'd seen her cheering on her teammates from the bench, seeing the way they'd all come over to her when they'd won, including her in the victory even though she'd been propped up on crutches.

He'd watched her with an American flag over her shoulders, her two teammates having taken her crutches and setting them to the side, propping her up and bringing her onto the ice so she could accept her medal.

Captivated.

He'd been at home, the league on a scheduled break, watching the game and . . . utterly captivated by Calle on TV.

Then fast-forward a few years, and they were both at the same organization.

And he was still as captivated.

He allowed himself one more glance to see she'd made it to her seat and had slung her backpack into the chair next to her. She had heavy circles beneath her eyes, and her skin was pale, almost gray.

Coop knew she was feeling sick again.

Shit.

As though she felt the weight of his stare, her eyes shot up to meet his. Then held, the moment stretching, her swallowing hard, concern and panic trailing across her face. What? Did she think he was going to come back there and confront her? After he'd gone through the effort of creating the ruse to put off Bernard?

He tried to communicate that through his eyes, but when all she did was break their connection and look down at her hands, Coop knew she didn't understand he wasn't going to push something, wasn't going to do anything to jeopardize her career.

Sighing, he shifted so he was facing forward, glancing down at his phone and cueing up his audiobook.

Another thing the guys would give him a hard time for.

His love of historical fiction romance novels.

On audio.

With dual narration.

Good lord, he was a moron.

But there was something about getting lost in a book that was so different from his present or past life, so completely different from anything he had ever experienced, that when Coop had unwittingly ordered and then started listening to one—instead of the thrillers he'd stuck with for most of his adult life—he'd been absolutely hooked.

Seemingly random societal rules, lots of clothing to fantasize removing from a woman—cough, *Calle*—horses and letters and—

His family would give him so much shit—both his biological and hockey ones.

But he'd always been a bit of a romantic. He enjoyed finding out the things the women in his life might want but would never ask for and then giving them freely. He sent flowers. He bought treats. He . . . wooed.

Oh, but thank fuck no one on the team could read his mind in that moment.

Wooed?

That would garner way more shit-giving than the car or popping a boner like a fifteen-year-old-kid.

Although . . .

His dad loved his mom, had won her over by pure dint of character and perseverance, and the paired-up guys on the team also loved their women. They freely sent gifts. They did PDA and phone calls and pet names. Hell, even Stefan had managed to renegotiate his and Brit's contracts to allow them to have a relationship and, not so long ago, Coop had watched PR-Rebecca yank a giant stuffed bear proclaiming Kevin's love of her brownies to the world on the equally over-sized heart it held down the hallway at the practice facility. And he'd heard loads about Mike and his quote-unquote Love Doctor abilities as to how he'd worn down his Sara with romance and stubbornness. Then later how he'd helped Blane with Mandy *and* Max with Angie. Not to mention, their trainer, Gabe, who'd won shy, Nutritionist-Rebecca's heart with his own special brand of persistence mixed with thoughtfulness.

So, he wasn't alone.

And also, now that he was thinking of all those scenarios and measuring them against one another, Coop wasn't sure if it was romance that had won out or stubbornness.

His lips twitched as he considered each in turn.

Stubbornness.

Yup, hands down. When it counted, his friends knew how to push and cajole and out-persist the women in their lives.

The rest of the time, they just sat back and enjoyed the ride.

Coop had always felt a little out of place, not because his teammates excluded him, but rather because he was one of the few single guys, and being around all of that paired-off happiness at team events was sometimes like a gut-punch.

He wasn't a bachelor by choice, necessarily.

He'd been in a long-term relationship with a woman before he'd been traded to the Gold, but they'd made the mutual decision that they weren't compatible enough to justify Hannah uprooting her life and moving away from her job and family to come to San Francisco.

So, they'd gone their separate ways in drama-free fashion, and Coop had been single.

Then he'd found out that Calle was going to be on the coaching staff.

He'd perked up, been excited to meet her.

Then he'd actually *met* her.

And suddenly, playing the field in SF hadn't seemed all that appealing. Yes, he'd gone out with the few single guys a couple of times, but the club scene hadn't ever really been his thing, and, honestly, no one had really been able to measure up to Calle. It wasn't like he'd fallen head over heels for her or fallen in love at first sight, but rather that image of her on TV had melded with her awesomeness in real life—not to mention the fact that she was beautiful and sexy and had a great smile—and . . . his standards had shifted. No other woman could compare or compete with this vision in his head, the vision in his mind was of a woman that was very much like Calle.

Except a Calle that wasn't his coach.

And he hadn't known how to go about finding her.

So, he'd kept his head down, his skates on the ice, his body in the training room, and his head in the game, hoping that this non-coach Calle would fall into his lap.

But that hadn't happened.

But *Coach* Calle kind of had.

Calle had.

The words of the audiobook drifted through his ears, but damn if Coop absorbed any of them.

Because all he could think was that Calle *had* fallen into his lap.

He knew about the baby. He'd gone to the doctor with her. They'd talked and shared and—

He wanted *her*.

Wonderful and kind, smart and talented, funny and fiery Calle.

But . . . he also didn't want to ruin either of their careers. Or overcomplicate her life when she was already dealing with an unexpected baby and the fallout from her ex.

What then?

The plane began taxiing down the runway, picking up speed before it lifted off the ground and took to the air. But as the plane flew through the darkened night sky, leveling off at thirty-thousand feet and heading for home, he realized he only had two options and that he needed to choose one of those two before he got back to San Francisco.

Did he back off? Bury everything he was feeling and ignore the chemistry between them? Move on with his life and try to find a woman who made his heart feel like Calle did?

Or . . . did he try to figure out a way to win Calle over? And further that, did he try to find a way to win her over while keeping both of their jobs secure?

He knew what he *wanted*.

But was what he wanted smart or safe or in either of their best interests?

And did she want *him?*

Well, she certainly kissed like she wanted him. She definitely shared the emotion of the moment at the ultrasound. She clearly enjoyed bantering and teasing him.

That was want.

Those were ties that had already woven them together.

Coop shifted in his seat, glancing back down the aisle. Calle was asleep in her chair, mask over her eyes, travel pillow tucked around her neck, head slumped slightly to the side. Her chest rose and fell in steady intervals, and her palm rested lightly on her abdomen. Her face was relaxed, though even in the dim illumination of the cabin's night lighting, he could still see she was pale.

A pulse of protectiveness wove through him.

And longing.

To walk down the aisle and slip into the seat next to her, to coax her to lie down in his lap and stroke his fingers through her hair until she fell back asleep, to cover that hand on her stomach with his own, to pretend the baby he'd seen on the ultrasound screen, the rapid *whoosh-whoosh* of its heartbeat still sounding in his ears belonged in some way to him.

Calle didn't need him, didn't need his help, nor his protection.

But that only made him want to give it more. In fact, he didn't know if he could exist in a world where he wasn't looking out for her, where he wasn't trying to discover all the little things he could do to make her smile, where he didn't have the right to hold her in his arms, to kiss and stroke and . . . love.

Which kind of made up Coop's mind for him, didn't it?

Calle was his.

She'd been his in some way or another since he'd seen her on TV, since he'd met her in real life.

Now, he needed to weave those connections tight.

To weave *himself* into them right alongside her.

He turned forward, eyes locking with Bernard's for a split second before he let his break away.

Yeah, he had work to do. He needed to woo her, to romance her, to make himself indispensable, and all along the way to weave them both tightly together so nothing could separate them.

Not her fear.

Not their jobs.

Not the baby.

Coop didn't want *anything* to separate them.

Unfortunately, it didn't occur to him during the short, quiet plane ride home that oftentimes wanting something didn't mean a damned thing.

He was certainly going to find out that was the case with Calle.

TEN

CALLE

"I have to tell you something," she announced, barging into Bernard's office in a move that was certainly rude but also made in desperation because she'd spent the morning upchucking at regular intervals in her office and knew that she needed to level with her boss.

It had been three days since Anaheim.

Four since the desk-time exploits with Coop in her office.

Well four since Coop's wonderful fingers, slightly calloused and broad, had slipped between her legs and found her clit without a roadmap, dropping into a rhythm that had sent her soaring with no little amount of confidence.

She stifled a shiver, knowing she'd have been called a liar if she hadn't said that she'd thought about that moment multiple times, that she'd dreamed and—

Not the moment for that particular mental minefield.

Bernard glanced up from his desk, stare heavy, face serious. "Coop?"

She frowned. "What?"

Silence.

One white brow came up. "Does the *something I need to tell you* involve Coop?"

"Um. No?" Or at least she didn't think it did. *Fuck.* Had he found out about the scene in her office? She'd been so careful to stay away from him, to make sure there couldn't be a single iota of her behavior that wasn't the least bit professional.

Except for coming on his fingers.

Except dreaming about it every moment since.

Except for thinking about it as she'd made herself come with her vibrator before going to sleep after returning from the airport, then again the next day, then again yesterday.

Pregnancy hormones were no joke.

Or maybe it was just Coop and the way her body always seemed to come alive when he was nearby, heat prickling down her spine, moisture pooling between her legs—

She opened her mouth, shut it again.

More silence. Then,

"Close the door," Bernard said.

She nodded, spun to push the wooden panel shut, then turned back around.

"Sit."

Another nod and she sat in the chair in front of his desk, mouth suddenly dry.

"Spill."

It was an order, and she'd been a member of a team for too many years of her life to not immediately open her mouth and spill.

"I'm pregnant."

"It's Coop's?"

Her jaw dropped open, gut twisting. "What? *No.*"

Calle had thought she'd done such a good job of pretending their interlude in the office hadn't happened, but clearly, she needed to be smarter and more distant. She sucked in a breath, released it slowly, trying to sort out her brain. "It's Jason's. He doesn't want anything to do with the baby. In fact, I just overnighted him papers to terminate his parental rights yesterday."

Bernard leaned back in his chair. "I see."

"I'm not due until late August," she said. "I know that's good for this season, though the timing is shit for the next one. If you and management renew my contract, that is," she hurried to add, knowing that this wasn't great information or something that would bolster her contract negotiations. "I'll make arrangements to get back to the team as quickly as possible and try not to miss any training camp or preseason games. I know it's important for us to work out the kinks in the roster and—"

She caught a glimpse of Bernard's face and stopped talking so quickly that her teeth clicked together audibly.

"Are you telling me," he said after a moment, "that the dumbass you used to date got you pregnant and now is willingly giving up you and his baby?"

Her chin dropped to her chest before looking up to meet Bernard's stare. "It's—" A shake of her head. "It's not like that. I mean. It was a one-off thing after we'd broken up. Jason wants to live his own life. I knew that and shouldn't have—" Another shake. "Well, I knew better and—"

"He was there, too."

Calle sighed. "Yes, he was. But I let him back into my life and now . . ." She crossed then uncrossed her legs. "I know it was a mistake, and I definitely don't want him involved, especially if he doesn't want to be. A father should want to be in a child's life, not—"

Be forced.

Fuck.

She broke off, smothering the words, smothering the memories.

Her father had been forced—her parents' union a product of a shotgun wedding, and her arrival the catalyst. Which begged the question of how she could have been so stupid to have gotten pregnant by a man who didn't want to be involved. But birth control. Fucking birth control that didn't always work. Or maybe fuck Jason and his sperm that had managed to power its way through.

Gross.

But more importantly, she was pregnant. She was keeping it and kicking Jason the fuck out. She and her baby didn't need to experience what she'd dealt with growing up. That little slice of unhappy hadn't been good for anyone in her father's sphere, but it had been worse for her mom, her, and her siblings.

Miserable.

No child should know they're unwanted.

She swallowed and placed her hand over her stomach, wanting to protect the tiny little being inside her from the feeling that had been so prevalent during her childhood.

Bernard saw her hand, but then again, her boss had never missed much.

His face softened.

She didn't want soft. She wanted to assure him that she wouldn't fuck up, that her job was important to her, that she wanted to be here and keep coaching. But before she could say any of those things, he stood, picking up a folder and extending it over the desk.

What was in it?

A pink slip?

They didn't actually give pink slips, did they? More likely, they'd talk to her agent and tell Devon that they weren't renewing her contract. The oldest Scott was a former player and ran Prestige Media Group, one of the best agencies in the country for athletes. He wouldn't let her get pink-slipped. Or if he couldn't prevent said pink-slipping, he'd at least give her some warning, especially when he'd told her everything was going well the last time they'd spoken and—

"Here."

Calle scrambled to her feet when Bernard waved the folder slightly, fingers grasping the edge.

He held firm to the other side, studied her closely.

After an interminable moment, his fingers opened, and she was the sole person holding the folder.

"It's your new contract offer," he said.

Her breath slid out, relief pouring through her. "Oh."

"PMG has received it as well, but I thought you might want a full copy, too, so I asked management for it." He came around the desk, clapped her shoulder lightly. "We wouldn't let you go because you were pregnant, Calle."

She lifted her chin. "I know that." Lie. Especially since she'd been thinking about pink slips ten seconds earlier.

"Did you?" His tone told her he'd known what she'd been thinking.

Nibbling on the corner of her mouth, she admitted. "No. Well, yes," she said. "I didn't think you'd directly fire me because I was pregnant . . . more like you'd find something wrong with my performance . . . so *then* you could let me go."

His brow lifted again and damn, but she'd always been jealous when people could do that. Her eyebrows only lifted in unison, so she couldn't perfect the penetrating look that Bernard wielded on a regular basis. But then he opened his mouth and spoke, and she forgot about eyebrows altogether.

"There's nothing wrong with your performance, Calle," he said. "And further that, we're a family here. I know my wife, for one, would love to babysit, seeing as how she was just telling me the other day that our own kids are completely helpless when it comes to producing grandchildren."

"I—"

"Also, I think you'll find it helpful for planning purposes to know that Mandy just got the approval for the team's day care facility. There will be sites at both the practice facility and here at the arena." He led her toward the door. "Though that doesn't cover road trips, it should bring you some peace of mind for when the team's in town."

Calle blinked, eyes suddenly burning.

Must be some dust in the air.

That was it.

"Thanks, Coach," she murmured, reaching for the doorknob, still blinking because aside from puking and being insanely turned on by a certain gorgeous forward, she was also ripe full of *all* the emotions.

He brushed her hand away, placed his palm on the door. "Calle?"

She glanced up. "Yeah?"

"It'll be okay."

A nod. "Yeah."

"Also"—she held her breath—"You feeling okay?"

One side of her mouth hitched up. So, maybe she didn't have eyebrow skills, but at least she had mouth skills . . . and okay, she took that back. Mouth skills sounded terrible and totally like something Mandy and Brit would give her a hard time for.

Hard.

Oy.

She shook her head, forcing her normally focused, but hormone-and-space-cadet-riddled brain to focus. *Seriously. Get it. Together.* "I'm fine," she said. "Thanks—"

"Not nauseous?"

Her expression revealed the truth before she did because Bernard smiled ruefully. "That good, huh?"

"I'm assured the end is in sight," she said. "I'm almost out of the first trimester."

"Speaking of that"—he dropped his hand but didn't back away—"We need to talk planning for practice and ice time, and what your doctor okays as well as what the insurance company and board say will fly for that and travel. I don't think we have any plans in place for what happens if a member of the coaching staff gets pregnant."

"My doctor said it's fine for now."

"Okay," he said, "but we'll still need to talk about it."

Shit, she thought, but, "Right," was all she said.

"Tomorrow, though," Bernard said. "I promised the wife I'd be home in time for dinner for a change."

"Don't want to mess that up."

He shook his head. "I figured out a while back that I was done with messing up and have focused on *making* up. Life is a lot more fun that way."

"Making up for what?"

A shadow crossed his expression, but then he smiled, and she knew she'd hit a raw spot. Before she could change the subject, he said, "Let's just say we men know when a woman is worth the effort, and my wife is that ten times over."

Calle nodded. "She's lucky to have you."

"The opposite is definitely true." His lips twitched. "Especially having to put up with an asshole like me."

"Ah," she said, wanting to lighten the moment further. "I see. You made her do extra off-ice workouts, didn't you?"

Bernard didn't miss a beat. "She can't stand the box jumps."

Calle laughed and reached for the knob again. "I'll bring you in a plan for practices and the like to talk about tomorrow."

A nod.

She tugged open the door.

"Calle?" She paused on the threshold, turned back. "Check out the clause on page eighteen." He nodded at the contract in her hands and she could have sworn there was a hidden smile in his eyes. But Bernard didn't smile, least of which with his eyes. "Just in case someone else decides to make up instead of fuck up."

Her brows drew together, but before she could ask, Bernard grabbed his jacket, cell, and wallet, then brushed past her.

"Shut that door, would you?" he called and took off down the hall.

She watched him go, contract gripped tight, confusion swarming through her.

That was when her cell rang.

She picked it up, swiped a finger across the screen, and held it up to her ear.

Devon's voice drifted through the speaker.

"What idiot on the Gold has managed to capture your heart?" he asked then paused. "And how painfully do I need to kill him?"

———

She sat in Devon's office, the handsome former hockey player—and cover model—pouring over the printout of the digital copy of her contract. He was comparing it to the one Bernard had handed her, going line by line, turning page after page until he finally glanced back up at her.

"It's the same," he said. "Word for word identical."

"And the clause on page eighteen?"

"You mean the clause that makes me want to murder whoever dared to put hands on you?"

"Devon," she warned.

They'd dated—briefly—when he'd been an up-and-coming rookie NHLer and she'd been new on the national team. He was quite a few years older, and that wasn't a surprise to her mental state at the time.

She'd been looking for a father figure.

Definitely not the right mindset for a newly eighteen-year-old girl, nor for a twenty-three-year-old man who was just starting his career. They'd been introduced through mutual friends, had gone on exactly two and a half dates—half, because they'd both realized it wasn't working then had moved on to being what they should have started off as: friends.

Devon had gone off to do great things in the league, then off it, including dating a bevy of beautiful models and founding Prestige Media Group, before marrying the wonderful Becca. Throughout the years, they'd stayed in touch and when he'd heard about her name being in the running for the position with the Gold, he'd offered to be her agent and negotiate the deal.

She'd accepted without reservation.

Because even though she and Devon might have never worked

out in the dating world, he was a good man. He'd called her after her devastating knee injury—which had happened on international broadcast during primetime—to offer her words of encouragement . . . and the name of a doctor who specialized in rehabbing professional athletes. And when rehabbing had failed, he'd continued calling, not letting her sink into what-should-have-beens and encouraging her to find a new path. Later, he'd helped her secure the opportunity of a lifetime when the occasion presented itself.

So, yeah, maybe they hadn't had sexual sparks, but he'd still protected her and been there for her. And maybe, if she were admitting it only to herself, had still become a bit of a father figure anyway.

His face at that moment was certainly giving her intensely disapproving fatherly vibes.

Probably why she was hesitant to admit the next.

"I'm pregnant."

A thundercloud crossed over his face. That was the only way she could think to describe it—eyes sparking like the precursor to lightning, a jaw that was tense as an impending tornado, words that clipped across the room like hail colliding with the roof of a car.

"I repeat. Who. Am. I. Going. To. Kill?"

"What exactly does that clause say?" she asked. She'd read the entire page eighteen and could barely make heads or tails of it. The language was filled with words like indemnifying and holding harmless and due diligence and while she knew what each of them meant individually, contract law wasn't her specialty.

He growled.

Calle wasn't cowed. Yes, they might be friends. No, she might not want to disappoint him. But also, *yes*, she'd seen him snort coffee through his nose on their third—well, second and a half—date when she'd declared they didn't have a chance in hell of making a relationship work between them. So, no, cowering didn't happen with this man. He'd spent the years making her feel safe and protected and not alone, and while she appreciated that, she also didn't need to be packed with cotton and stored safely away from trouble brewing on the horizon.

This was her job. Her life. Her future.

She had it.

"Devon."

His eyes narrowed. "Who?"

She sighed. "It's Jason's baby, Dev. None of the guys on the team are involved." *Lie,* her brain reminded her. *Coop is involved.* Except, Coop *wasn't* involved. Because it wasn't his baby.

But you want him to be, her brain said in a nah-nah-nah-nah tone.

Shit.

She *did* want that.

Forcing the mental dialogue away, she looked back up at Devon. "Jason doesn't want anything to do with the baby. I've talked to a lawyer and sent him paperwork to terminate his rights. He told me he would sign," she said and watched the thundercloud transform into a lightning storm on Dev's face. His eyes filled with such fire that she could imagine bolts of electricity hurling themselves across the room, reducing innocent furniture to charred wood. "And before you say you're going to kill him, know that I don't want Jason in my life. Our . . . time together was a mistake." She shook her head. "He was in town for Thanksgiving, and I was lonely and—" Her words broke off because—

So. Fucking. Stupid.

But then she thought of the fluttering heart on the monitor, the tiny arms and legs, and her palm came up, pressed lightly to her stomach. This was her chance to make sure the past didn't repeat itself. Her baby was never going to feel unwanted or like a burden. No matter what.

"I knew I should have made you come to Thanksgiving dinner with me and Becca."

Calle's lips quirked. "That might have been too many Scotts, even for me."

"You should have been there. You could have judged Kelsey's"
—his younger sister, who was Calle's age—"boyfriend."

"You said Tanner was a good guy."

And apparently Kels had led Tanner on quite a chase.

"He is," Devon said, grudgingly. "Plus, she's happy."

This was so much better, to have the conversation focused on
Dev rather than her. "Then why do you sound like you've swallowed glass?"

He made a face. "Tanner was Bas"—his younger brother—
"and my friend. He's too old for her and it's . . ."

"You're protective."

Dev didn't comment.

She reached across the desk, patted his hand. "That's what
makes you a good guy, Dev. Also," she added with a teasing lilt to
her words. "I seem to remember you dating a younger girl once.
One who was your younger sister's age."

He wrinkled his nose. "Sometimes it's not fair that you've
known me for almost a decade."

"Yes, it is," she said. "I get to have all the dirt." A beat. "Like
why you never drink iced coffee anymore.

He snorted, shook his head. "You've always been relentless."

"I seem to remember a certain Scott showing me the definition of relentless."

"That was on the ice," he said, sitting back in his chair. "Now
that I'm retired to the boring world of contracts and negotiating
deals, I'm much more relaxed."

"Oh sure," she said, mirroring him and leaning back in her
own seat, while waving a hand lazily up and down his muscled
frame. "You've clearly relaxed in the gym"—he was more built
than she'd ever seen him—"and in your professional life"—
nothing like building up PMG to be the top name in the
industry.

"First," he said. "Jasper"—his infant son—"is a night owl, like
his dad, and he'll only sleep if I keep him next to me while I'm on
the bike—"

"And while you're lifting weights?" she interjected because no one got a body like Devon's by solely riding a stationary bike.

He ignored her.

"—and PMG is only the top agency in the country because I have the best people working for me."

That right there.

That was why a small part of her wished that she and Dev had worked out. He was the kind of man she'd want in her baby's life.

She glanced down at her lap, knowing she was being ridiculous.

They never would have worked, and she wasn't just going to jump into a relationship with someone solely so her baby could have a good dad. That had disaster written all over it.

Plus, she had this.

She didn't need anyone. She'd figure it out and—

Fuck. Okay, she didn't have this.

Calle knew absolutely nothing about babies. She'd held Jasper all of one time, and the kid had cried for five straight minutes until Becca had taken pity on her and swooped in.

Could the baby just stay at the hospital until he or she was say . . . five?

She knew how to deal with five-year-olds.

And yes, she was well-aware of how absolutely insane she sounded. But she was *going* insane. She and Jason and the one-night stand. Her and Coop and what had happened in her office. Work and a contract that made Dev want to kill something.

It felt like someone had taken all the individual pieces of her life, shoved them into a snow globe, and then had shaken the lot of them into a jumbled mess. Sighing, she rubbed her forehead, knowing that the stinging in her eyes was more because she was hormonal than from actual tears.

She didn't cry . . . except at SPCA commercials. That music—

A hand on her shoulder.

"Hey," Dev said, shaking her lightly, waiting to speak again until her eyes met his. "It'll be okay."

"I'm not so sure of that," she admitted. "I'm a mess and . . . I don't even know where to start or how to navigate this."

His fingers squeezed lightly. "Welcome to your first lesson in parenthood," he said, lightly. "None of us know what the fuck we're doing."

"You and Jas—"

"I was afraid I was going to break him the first time I held him." His lips curved at what was no doubt an incredulous expression on her face. "It's true," he said, holding up his battle-worn hands. They were calloused and scarred and very similar to her own. "You know it took Becca a long time to get pregnant and when she was, I worried something would go wrong or that she would lose it again. Then when he was safely here, I was worried these mitts would do something wrong, but it's more than that. I spent so much time worrying about every decision, about everything I did, that I almost forgot to enjoy each step of the journey."

"What changed?" she asked.

"Becca." His expression warmed, all of the stormy emotions gone at the mention of his wife. "She set me straight. She's never had a problem with knocking me around"—Calle's lips twitched, knowing the sweet and gentle Becca would never do such a thing —"but what really got my head out of my ass was when she said, 'We have plenty of money to pay for Jas's therapy, so stop worrying about everything.'"

Calle's brows rose, unsure if he was serious. "Um . . . that's a good thing?"

"Well, technically, she yelled it," Dev said.

Calle's brows dropped back down. "She *yelled* it?" Becca was on the quiet side, and it was hard to picture her yelling at all, especially at her husband, who worshipped the ground she walked on.

Dev nodded. "Yup."

"Damn. Go, Becca."

He snorted. "That's what Kels said." A roll of his eyes. "But the point stands, I was stressed and worried for nothing—and I'm not saying don't prepare or read or take the classes—but just know that you'll find your way, the one that works for you and your baby. And further that, Calle, you're not alone. You have people who love you. Not just the team but also the team of Scotts. You know that my mom will be all over babysitting."

Her throat was tight. "That was what Bernard said about his wife."

"I'm happy to referee as they battle it out." Dev released her arm, tugged the end of her ponytail. "Plus, we've got a house full of way too much baby shit, and by the time your little one comes, we'll get you stocked up on the big things. You'll hire a nanny for when you're with the team—"

"They're starting a day care at the practice facility and the arena."

"Good." Dev stood. "When's the baby due?"

"End of August," she said.

"Perfect timing," he said, eyes calculating. "You can coach through the season, have the baby over the summer and come back before the season starts in October."

"But training camp and preseason—"

"The schedule is lighter then, and there are ways to see both. Maybe something virtual. You can watch a feed from home. Or attend as much as you're comfortable with. I'm sure we can negotiate some terms."

She sucked in a breath and nodded.

"You'll get stuff done step by step. Dealing with what needs to be sorted now and leaving the later stuff until later."

"O-okay." She was trying to look business-like and put together, but all of those pesky hormones were rearing their heads, and she was feeling very emotional.

Luckily, Dev seemed to realize that because he rounded his desk, sat back into the plush leather chair, and then picked up the contract. "This contract offer is for five years, Calle. That's huge."

"*What?*"

"Five years and—" He named a figure that she hadn't looked at because she'd been too focused on page eighteen. "Along with bonuses for making the playoffs and how far the team goes. More if the team wins the Cup again."

She blinked, trying to process what he'd just laid out.

"So, first steps, Bernard knows, but not the board?"

A nod.

"Okay," he said, "so the offer is more than generous and will give you the stability to plan ahead. My advice is you should sign."

"Shouldn't they know about the pregnancy first?"

"No," he said. "You're not required to tell them, and you're technically a protected class. You intend to fulfill your end of the contract, so we should get the big details locked in, then you and the doctor need to figure out what you'll do on the ice and for how long—"

"The doctor says I can stay on ice for another month to start, and then we'll talk."

"That makes sense, though the insurance company will probably make the final call on that when you tell the organization." He tapped a finger to his lips. "That's fine, we'll deal with it. Plenty of coaches don't spend a lot of time on the actual ice. We can get you a prime seat on the bench."

"Neither of us have ever liked warming the bench," she grumbled, even knowing he was right.

"But we paid our dues when we had to."

She smiled. "True." A beat. "Do you think Bernard will object to me rolling out a recliner to the ice?"

He grinned. "I think you keep making the offense play like they've been doing, and they'll bring you a throw blanket to keep your tootsies warm."

Calle burst out laughing then sighed. "I need to tell the board."

"You will. Sign everything tonight, protect yourself and your baby. Then tell them."

"It feels a little shady to spring it on them like that."

"You said you told Bernard. Did he care?"

"No," she admitted. "I told him, he reassured me, and then gave me the contract."

"I'm guessing if he had concerns, we would have heard from the board already."

True.

They *had* been here for—she glanced at the clock—nearly five hours. Ample time to inform the board and rescind the offer.

Also, *shit*. They'd been here for five hours. It was nearly ten.

She needed to let him get home, back to Becca and Jasper. That, along with the rest of it, propelled her past the rest of the reservations, and she gave her assent. They spent the next little while, going over the pages, Dev explaining everything, before she digitally signed the offer and was under contract for the next five years.

He hugged her as she stood and gathered her things. "You got this."

"I have this," she agreed, feeling slightly more confident because Dev believed in her.

He walked her to the door.

"Good thing you got that two-bedroom, huh?"

"That is true," she murmured. "Almost like I planned it."

A tug to her ponytail. "Don't be a stranger," he said softly. "And call Becca, she'd love to talk pregnancy with someone. You should probably start looking for a nanny. Full-time ones can be hard to find."

Ice-time plan. Call Becca for pregnancy details. Nanny.

She straightened her shoulders, feeling better to have some sort of plan.

"Take it one step at a time, and you can do this, honey."

For the first time, she thought she could.

Calle walked out the door, remembered what she'd forgotten, and turned back, asking, "Oh, by the way, I still don't get what's so important about page eighteen."

A ghost of a smile crossed Dev's face.

"Page eighteen gives you the freedom to date one of the Gold players if you both consent and let HR know."

Her jaw dropped open. "*What?*"

Dev nodded. "Anyone come to mind?"

Someone *did* come to mind. Someone who was definitely *not* involved in any of those plans she and Devon had just come up with. Devon . . . who was now staring at her with a considering expression and one brow raised.

Fucking people and the one-brow-raises.

That someone was Coop.

H. E. Double hockey sticks.

ELEVEN

COOP

He might have made some big decisions on the plane ride home, but that didn't mean Calle was receptive to them.

In fact, she hardly seemed to *see* him at all over the next couple of weeks.

She was never alone at the rink, or the practice facility, or anywhere where he might have a minute to talk to her by herself. There always seemed to be an important conversation taking place with either Bernard or Mandy or one of the other players.

But not with him. *Never* with him.

She spoke with Blue. With Brit. With Stefan. With Max. With every other fucking player.

But not him.

Two weeks and the only time she'd been forced to communicate with him at all was during the games . . . and she made sure to do that alongside another player.

It was deftly done, so easily excising him from her life.

The move still pissed Coop off.

She'd let him in, just slightly, given him a glimpse of what the possibility of them might look like, and then, in one instant, she'd taken it away.

He felt like stomping his foot, demanding *It isn't fair!*

Then he pulled his head out of his ass.

Because seriously, his mom would kill him if she caught one whiff of what was going through his head. As though he had any bearing on what Calle chose to do with her life, or whether she decided to let him into it. It was arrogant. Pushy—

His dad would probably approve.

Coop snorted and bent to tie his skates.

Lots of people he knew came from divorced parents or broken families. Which wasn't a surprise, he supposed, since half of marriages ended in divorce. But he'd grown up with happily married parents in a middle-class household. His mom was a teacher, his dad, a manager at a car dealership. There had been plenty of love and support and while they hadn't had an extra two hundred dollars to spend on the newest pair of Jordan's, Coop had always known he was safe with his family, that would be food in the fridge, and his parents would always be there for him.

That had changed somewhat as he'd gotten older—when he'd been followed around a store by a clerk certain he was going to steal something, just because his skin was darker than theirs, or pulled over and stopped for no reason when driving to a friend's house that happened to be white.

It was a strange and infuriating dichotomy at times, knowing that he could be as successful as he was and still be reduced to a color.

But his parents had always been frank with him, laying out reality in a way that had scared him shitless as a teenager moving to another state to live with another family—who happened to be white—and that frankness had given him the tools to navigate a world where he was often judged because of his skin.

Coop was well-aware it shouldn't have to be that way, but he also wasn't delusional. Changes might be coming to the world they all lived in, albeit far too slowly, but that judgment didn't just disappear on a whim.

Sighing, he switched to the other skate, thinking about all the times he'd been discriminated against, knowing that he was luckier than many of the kids he'd grown up with. But that didn't change reality, and the problems in society didn't go away, no matter how much money he made.

But he also didn't think that *this* situation with Calle was about his race. They'd been together two seasons, and he would have seen something before if it was.

Instead, he thought she was running scared.

Case in point, she'd just walked into the locker room, taken one look at him then dropped her eyes to her feet and hurried across the space to Blue.

Yup. This distance was because he'd gotten too close.

And she was going to do what she had to do to keep that barrier in place.

Like his mom had with his dad.

Family history told a winding tale of his dad's attempted courtship with his mom throwing up roadblocks every step of the way. She'd had a bad childhood, had come from a broken home and it had left deep, heavy scars. But his dad had seen what was beneath and he'd pushed, shoved, cajoled and romanced, and then pushed and shoved some more to weave his way into his mom's heart.

"It was all worth it," his dad had told Coop on numerous occasions. "Nothing truly worthwhile is easy. Whether it's hockey or a good woman." This was often accompanied by a firm clap on the shoulder and, "Learn to tell the difference between cotton candy and a Snicker's bar. Both taste good, but only one has substance."

Well, he'd seen Calle. He'd *tasted* Calle.

He knew she wasn't cotton candy.

She was a fucking Snicker's bar, and he wanted to devour every last bite.

He just needed to figure out how to undo the wrapper.

———

Operation opening the wrapper commenced during practice by taking a page out of his dad's book at practice a few days later. The team had been off for the weekend and now were back at the rink, prepping for an extended road trip with a couple of practices and then flying out in two days.

And by taking a page out of his dad's book, Coop basically meant being a pushy, pain in the ass until he managed to get through that outer wrapping of Calle's.

As with most of the other teams Coop had played for, the Gold were given the drills beforehand, and they were expected to come to practice prepared to roll so the coaches could focus on solving big team issues rather than chalk-talking skating and passing drills. If a player had a specific skill or issue to resolve, that was generally done before or after practice when all the guys had free access to the ice. Or, if it was a larger problem, then players took it upon themselves to secure additional time separate of the team's slots

Coop had done this a few times over the years, once after a groin pull had wreaked havoc on his skating stride and he'd needed the help of a skating guru—a former professional figure skater who was well-known for being able to break down the minutia that went into a player's stride. She'd been tough as hell, but part of the reason his skating was better now than it had ever been. Another time, he'd arranged extra practice when he was really struggling to pick up a new system and knew he needed to get his shit together or he might end up not playing.

But he hadn't needed to do that with the Gold.

Until now.

He found that he was suddenly very confused by Calle's new offensive play and needed some extra help . . . in the form of a private lesson.

Or maybe private lessons.

Of course, said private lesson would be a whole lot better if he could swing it *off* the ice, but for now, he'd settle for her just looking at him, for just a few moments of that pretty gaze where he tried to communicate to her that if she shed that outer protective layer around herself, she would still be safe.

The question was, *how* to do that?

She was worried about her job.

He was, too, for that matter—though it was probably horribly irresponsible that it wasn't the thing he was *most* worried about. In fact, Calle topped his list of concerns. He stewed over how she was feeling, wondered if he could finagle a way to go to her next appointment or how pissed she would be if he just showed up. He wanted to find out if Jason had really relinquished his rights and then track down the other man and tear him to pieces no matter what he'd ultimately decided.

Because he'd hurt Calle.

But for this moment, Coop knew that he had to play it smart and easy and . . . persistent. She needed to keep seeing him, and he needed to find ways to make it so she couldn't ignore him.

He waited until practice was over, until after the individual groups had come together for a quick chat at center ice. That talk was now breaking up as the guys headed to the locker room to shower and change and thus, it was the perfect opportunity to ask, "Calle, I have a question about that positioning in the corner. Can you show me again?"

Blue, heading toward the door leading off the ice, glanced back at him, expression incredulous, knowing damn well Coop didn't have any questions about the play.

So, perhaps he wasn't the smoothest when it came to getting Calle alone.

Probably, it would start talk in the locker room, and he'd soon be facing the nth degree from Brit and company.

But he had to start somewhere, and the safest place seemed to be on the ice.

Calle had been avoiding him for three weeks now, but he'd used the time to figure out his head, to cement what he'd really known all along—that Calle was the woman for him. He didn't care that she was pregnant by someone else, didn't care that she was his coach, didn't care that he was risking his job.

Calle was more important.

And he'd be lying if he said the baby in her womb didn't already feel a bit like his. He'd heard the heartbeat, seen the image. The tie was already there, and there was no going back.

Now, he just needed to convince Calle of that fact.

At his question, she glanced toward the bench, as though the open door could pull her through it, but then she visibly straightened her shoulders, lifted her chin, and nodded, as the rest of the team left. "Okay."

"I was wondering about . . ." he said, trailing off as he closed the distance between them, his eyes flicking toward the side, and the rest of the team leaving. Bernard was there, and the head coach gave him an assessing look, though it wasn't disapproving.

He made a mental note to have a conversation with him, and also with PR-Rebecca, if he managed to get Calle not to run away from him every time he was within ten feet.

"Wondering what?" she asked, words sharp.

Coop's gaze drifted the other way, noticing that while the stands were mostly emptied out—today's practice had been open to the public to come watch—there were still a few fans in the stands.

Time would tell if the audience made her feel more or less comfortable.

"I was wondering what you'd recommend for body positioning if the puck comes out that way—" He pointed with his stick.

Deep chocolate eyes on his. "You're full of shit."

He nodded. "I am."

She slipped off her glove and brushed a strand of hair off her face. But then she sighed and asked, "What do you want, Coop?"

"To make sure you're okay."

Amongst other things.

But—no pun intended—baby steps.

Another sigh, her eyes drifting over his shoulder and her jaw visibly tightening. "I'm fine."

He pointed with his stick again because don't let it be said he didn't take a ruse to its full potential. "Not sick still?" he asked. "The nausea is better?" He hadn't seen or come across her getting sick in the last few weeks, but that didn't mean she hadn't gotten better at hiding it.

"I want to sigh again," she said, "but I'm worried I'm going to turn into a moody teenager if I do."

He grinned. "I like you, moody or not."

"Forget it." She sighed for a third time. "I'm fine, Coop. I've got this under control"—he opened his mouth—"and yes, before you ask again, the nausea is better. The trip to Anaheim was the worst of it."

She was telling him the truth. He knew her well enough by now to recognize that.

"What's next?" he asked.

"If I tell you, will you chill out with the protectiveness?" she asked. "Because I swear, every time I turn a corner, you're there waiting for me to collapse."

More like having scoped out all available trash cans and ready to thrust it under her mouth at the slightest sign of pale skin or imminent vomiting. Not that he was going to mention that in this moment.

He might not be smooth.

But he wasn't fucking stupid.

However, he also wasn't going to promise to not protect her. Calle was his. And maybe she didn't know it yet, but that was going to change, and—

She was looking at him for an answer.

"I'm not waiting for you to collapse."

The look she shot him was dark enough that he should have

felt its physical impact right in the balls. "I'm not sick. I'm not tired. I've signed a five-year deal, and the board, as well as Bernard, know about the pregnancy."

Good. That was all good.

"And Jason?"

A roll of her eyes, but the action didn't hide the layer of hurt there. What Coop didn't know was whether the hurt was because she was missing the asshole or just from general sadness that her kid's bio dad was a douche who would never play the role of father properly.

"He signed the papers," she said. "My lawyer received them yesterday." Her eyes dropped to the ice. "I will admit I'm feeling a little guilty to be relieved. I want my baby to have a dad, just not one that will flit in and out of his life when it's convenient. I had that, and it—" She made a face. "Let's just say, it wasn't the greatest." One more long sigh then eyes up, chin up, placid expression on her face. "Okay, now I've allowed you the one heart-to-heart conversation you're going to get. Let's go back to you forgetting I'm pregnant until the rest of the team knows."

Yeah, no. That wasn't going to happen.

"His?" he asked as she started skating to the bench. He followed her obviously and so got to see the façade slip slightly, the softness gentling her features. "I thought your appointment wasn't for another week. You went back to the doctor and found out already?"

Calle shook her head. "No," she said. "I might be able to find out at my next appointment, something about the angle of the dangle—" She made a face. "Which sounds like a porn film, but it's not a hundred percent, and so I won't know for sure until I have my twenty-week ultrasound."

Coop made a mental note to download some baby books after he talked to Bernard and PR-Rebecca. He needed to know about things like ultrasounds and angles of the dangles—which coincidentally *did* sound like the name for a bad porn movie.

"So why him?"

She stepped off the ice. "Just feels like a *him*, I guess."

He followed Calle down the hall. "I can picture it. A rambunctious little brown-haired boy with mischievous chocolate eyes and boundless energy."

Her feet slid to a stop. "What are you doing, Coop?"

Why did she sound pissed?

"I'm just talking," he said carefully.

"No," she snapped, rounding on him. Even if he hadn't been able to hear her, he definitely would have known she was pissed, those pretty chocolate eyes sparked with annoyance, and a muscle ticked in her jaw. "What you're *doing* is trying to insert yourself into my life without me wanting it. Asking about the baby and my appointment schedule. Worrying about whether I'm feeling sick. Going behind my back and changing my contract offer so I can date you without consequence." She rapped her stick on the floor. "It's too fucking much, and you need to stop it now. I'm your coach. That's it. That's *all* it will ever be."

Okay, there was a lot to unpack with that statement.

But he couldn't focus on her words in that moment, not when she'd stepped closer, not when her body was a mere hairsbreadth from his, and not when he could smell her.

Fuck, he loved the way she smelled.

His fingers ached to reach out and grab hold of her.

She turned away and tossed her gloves into the bin that lined the hallway. Their equipment manager would take care of laundering and drying them, but he was hardly thinking of Richie in that moment. Because a moment after he followed Calle's lead, dumping his gloves into the bin as well, she whipped around and jabbed her finger into his chest.

He barely felt it, of course, not with all of his equipment on.

But he also *seriously* felt it, as though that simple press of her fingertip had seared through the layers of padding and fabric, of tissue and muscle and bone, and seared her touch on his soul.

"Stay out of my life," she gritted, her chest coming in rapid rises and falls. "I'm not in the market for another here-again-gone-tomorrow asshole who thinks he can control me."

"First," he said, stepping closer, capturing that finger in his hand, tugging her flush against him. "I'm not a here-again-gone-tomorrow type of man. I see something I like, and I go after it." He dropped his head, inhaling the scent of her hair and feeling his cock grow uncomfortably hard inside the cup he wore. "And I follow it through to the end." She shuddered when he placed his palm on the side of her neck.

"Second, I'm not trying to control you, Calle. I *like* you. I want you in my life so we can explore this draw between us. I've never met a woman I want to be with more, and that's not just because you're beautiful, but also because you're smart and funny and talented."

Her mouth dropped open and, mutely, she shook her head.

"It's true," he whispered. "I saw you during the gold medal game, saw you cheering on your team and then how they included you afterward. I knew then you were a good person and a good teammate."

"Coop—"

"Then I followed your career, happy when I saw your name popping up in different coaching circles, thrilled they were getting to be bigger and bigger opportunities." He cupped her cheek. "I didn't really know you, but I, like the rest of America, felt like I did, and I wanted you to succeed."

She sucked in a breath.

"And when you came to this team, when I knew you'd be coaching, I was fucking over the moon. I knew you'd be great. I just didn't know I'd end up falling for you and trying to pretend I hadn't for two solid years."

Silence.

"I don't know what the deal with the contract is," he said. "All I know is I promised myself I'd leave you alone, and even though I'm failing at that, you have to believe me when I say, I definitely didn't go over your head." He willed her to see the truth. "I would *never* do anything to affect your career, especially not in that way."

More silence.

Then, "I know."

He relaxed. "Good. I like you, sweetheart. Not for any other reason than you're absolutely incredible."

She inhaled sharply and neither of them said anything further. Calle's eyes were still on his, delving deeply, as though they could judge the truth of his words, if only she stared long or hard enough. She rose on tiptoe, bringing their mouths so close together that the barest movement on his part would align their lips.

But Coop didn't move, instinctively knowing that he'd made a move, he'd laid out his cards, that he'd pressed and pushed and now she needed the space to take the next step. Her lids closed, her body melted against his, and he still didn't unfreeze, even going so far as to hold his breath.

Her tongue darted out, moistening the lush pink bottom lip.

Fuck, he wanted to suckle on that lip, to have his against it, to run his tongue over it.

Patience.

Persistence.

Patien—

Her lips brushed his.

Heat exploded down his spine, and his mouth took on a life of its own, lips parting, tongue delving deeply into her mouth.

He didn't give her a nice kiss, or a gentle one. He wasn't sweet or easy. He brought every single technique of his teeth and tongue and lips to ramp her desire up so high that she'd want to keep on kissing him even as the world fell apart around them.

Eventually—needing oxygen was a fucking pain—he lifted his head, allowing them to both suck in some much-needed air.

"I think that kiss alone says that we need to find a way to explore what's between us, love," he murmured, lightly tracing his thumb across her bottom lip. "I've never felt anything like how I feel when I'm with you."

A shake of her head, lips still parted as she breathed rapidly. "It's just hormones. I—"

He kissed her again, long and deep and with plenty of tongue. When he pulled back, cupping her jaw in his palm, he held her eyes. "Not just hormones."

"I gained eight pounds," she blurted instead of agreeing with him. "I already gained eight pounds, and I'm going to be a disgusting, fat cow by the time I push this baby out, and you're *you,* and I'm—"

Coop decided the best way to progress this conversation along was to just keep kissing her.

So, he did.

At least until his lungs were screaming and she was nearly limp against him. "You're beautiful," he murmured then hurried to ask when that made her frown, "Go on one date with me?" He wanted her willing and pliable, not arguing with him over her appearance. So, he added, "Just *one* date. We'll stop if it's horrible, and no one will be the wiser."

She nibbled on her bottom lip and nodded.

"Tomorrow night?" he asked. "I'll pick you up at seven?"

More nibbling, but also, more nodding. "Okay."

His heart could have fucking burst from his chest, her answer gave him so much joy, but before he could kiss her again, before he could take just one more taste, Bernard appeared around the corner.

The coach didn't blink, not even when Calle quickly stepped away.

"Can I borrow you for a minute?" Bernard asked Calle.

She shot a look over her shoulder at Coop, bit her lip again, which made him really want to tug her close again and kiss the shit out of her. But he'd gotten her to agree to a date, so he wasn't going to blow it now.

"Thanks for the help," he said.

She nodded and hurried off down the hall.

Bernard followed her, sending an assessing look Coop's way and . . . had he just nodded approvingly? That was . . . really weird.

But Coop didn't have time to focus on the oddness surrounding the head coach.

He had a date to plan.

One during which he'd bust out every fucking play in the romance and wooing playbook that he knew or could think of.

One he'd make the best first date ever.

One he'd make so great that Calle would agree to go on another. And then another. And then *another*, until she was so wooed and romanced and tied to him that she'd never let him go.

TWELVE

CALLE

This was a huge mistake.

A giant mistake.

She never should have agreed to go on a date with Coop. *Never*.

But the man had kissed her—well, technically *she'd* started it. But the point was, he'd been standing there slightly sweaty and totally yummy, the spicy masculine scent of him surrounding her, his eyes so gentle and warm.

And she'd wanted just a taste of that warm.

A taste of him.

He'd given her that taste all right, and enough of it to turn her brain to mush and make her agree to stupid shit.

Like dates.

Which brought her to that evening.

The night before the team left for their road trip and she was standing in front of her closet, surveying the contents.

And finding them sorely lacking, it had to be noted.

She was going on a first date with a man who was totally inappropriate for her, and who also was the first man in her life where a first date meant a whole lot more than splitting the check over a mediocre dinner and a couple of cocktails.

For one, it wasn't a cheat day on Nutritionist Rebecca's plan.

For two, this was a date with *Coop*.

And she'd gained eight pounds. And already going into it, she had exactly one outfit that was worthy-enough-for-a-first-date-with-Coop—which meant it was sexy and not a T-shirt and sweats or a pair of fancy slacks and button-down she wore to the games. *And* in that one outfit, the shirt was too tight and the pants wouldn't button because . . . she'd gained eight fucking pounds.

She was going to be a behemoth.

A whale.

Floors were going to collapse under her feet.

Her skates were going to sink right through the ice to the sand beneath the paint.

Never mind that most of the guys still outweighed her by a good forty pounds, even with the eight-pound weight gain. Calle wasn't in the mood to be logical. She was in an absolute tizzy—scared and excited about the date, with a dash of *how-can-you-possibly-think-this-is-a-good-idea?* thrown in.

And she was in sweats.

And a T-shirt.

Because nothing else fit.

"Get it together, Stevens," she muttered, shoving one hanger after the other over the rack. "He's seen you in sweats too many times to count. Thus, he must like you in sweats. Thus *thus*"—yes, she was well-aware she was slowly going insane—"you should not be freaking out about something as stupid as an outfit when you're pregnant with another man's baby and trying to figure out your life, your career, and who will be the best nanny to trust with said baby because it's already terrifying to think about leaving him or her and—" She dropped her chin to her chest, blinking back tears. Again. For the hundredth time in the last few days, it seemed.

She'd switched nausea for crying fits, apparently, and could honestly say she didn't know which was worse.

"And it's going to be okay."

That statement didn't come from her.

In fact, it came from someone male and someone very much *not* her and . . . it came from Coop, okay?

She shrieked, hands incongruously moving to cover herself, even though she was fully dressed. "Coop! What the fuck? How did you get inside?"

He shrugged, though chagrin drifted across his face. "The door was unlocked."

Calle's brows drew together. "It was?"

A nod. "It was. Gotta be more careful, sweetheart."

Yeah, she did. But also, "Why didn't you knock?" She'd known he was going to pick her up. He'd said as much, and she'd known he hadn't asked for her address because he had followed her to her place after the first doctor's appointment. But she also didn't expect him to barge in and make himself at home.

That wasn't very Coop like.

"I did knock," he said. "Several times. Texted, too." *Oh.* She nibbled at her lip. "Also, I happen to like you in sweats," he added, pushing off the doorframe where he'd apparently been leaning, while watching her meltdown and talk to herself and—

He took her in his arms.

"I don't care that you're pregnant," he murmured, pulling her closer and resting his chin on the top of her head. It was a sign of how off-kilter she felt that she let him hold her.

Calle didn't hold her tongue, however. "You're going to care in six months' time, when I come home with a crying baby and a broken vagina from pushing him or her out."

Coop snorted. "I think your vagina will be fine. And if not, I have the funds to buy you a labiaplasty."

Her arms might have naturally looped around his waist when he'd taken her in his arms, but that didn't mean she was going to let him slide with the snark. Thus—dear Lord more *thuses*—she smacked him.

On his glorious ass.

Because hockey players had the best asses.

Yes, that was a bit egotistical since she was a hockey player herself, but it was true. Hockey players did *all* the squats and box jumps and biking and because of that, they carried a special brand of junk in the trunk.

Which meant when she smacked Coop's ass, the light swat quickly transformed into a light squeeze.

Then a not-so-light one.

She groaned.

He groaned.

"Going on a date with you is probably the stupidest thing I've ever done," she blurted, explaining when a slice of darkness slid across his expression. "My life is a barely controlled disaster. You should be out with some hot, single girl who isn't looking for nannies or spending hours arguing with the team's insurance company to get permission to stay on ice until I reach the third trimester or who's trying to plan her return to work after I've had the baby who's going to ruin my vagina and—"

He kissed her.

Not softly, either.

His lips dropped to hers, and he kissed her in a frenzy of teeth and tongue, demanding a response, effectively distracting her from her tizzy.

"I'd be arguing with you, too," he muttered, pulling back.

"What?" She blinked, desire had pooled in her center, and she was much more focused on getting Coop's mouth back on hers than their previous conversation.

"About being on the ice."

The fog began to clear, and she sighed, pushing lightly to get him to drop his arms. Which he didn't because . . . of course, he didn't. "Not you, too," she said. "I've been skating since I was three. Plus, I'm not playing. I'm observing."

"And you can't observe from the bench?"

Since this particular sentiment had been pointed out by the insurance agent and then Devon and *then* Becca when she'd called in her friend's wife for moral support—which, by the way, she *hadn't* gotten and instead had received words of caution, reminding her she had her whole life to skate and that she could accommodate a few months from the bench because one never knew what could happen and—

"You're about to yell at me, aren't you?" Coop asked.

"Yes!" She huffed, pushed at his arms again.

Again, he didn't let go.

"I'm not going to tell you what to do," he said. "It's your life —*and your baby's*—I know you'll make the right call to keep him or her safe."

She stopped. "You do?"

He nodded. "I do."

"And you're not going to give me shit about getting on the ice?"

"You've already made your decision," he said. "And I'm guessing you cleared it with all of the proper channels." He paused, and she nodded. "So no, I'm not going to give you a hard time. I think you know where I stand, and I hope you'll be open to revisiting the idea as things progress, but it's your body, sweetheart."

Her anger slid away.

"Though," he said, his hand coming up to brush her hair out of her eyes. "If you even think about demonstrating that move on the boards until that baby is safely outside your body"—his jaw hardened—"then I reserve the right to cart your ass off the ice."

"That seems fair," she said.

"Good."

He dropped his head again and slanted his lips across hers, kissing her until her lungs ached and her knees shook.

"This isn't really a first date, is it?" she asked when he pulled back, and after she'd caught her breath.

"No," he murmured, mouth trailing along her jaw.

Nothing about their relationship—was it a relationship?—felt normal. Not the chemistry, not the connection she felt to him. It was like the moment he'd overheard her on the phone, the moment he'd found out she was pregnant, everything had changed.

That last thought made her pause. Then consider.

Then . . . stiffen and say with horror, "Oh God, you're some sort of pervert who's only attracted to pregnant women, aren't you?"

Coop's head flew up, eyes wide, shock filling his face.

But then his lips twitched, and his arms dropped from around her waist. She didn't like that at all, but more she didn't like the fact that she'd discovered why he was suddenly so into her.

Normally, she'd be all about letting the freak flags fly.

But not when it involved her and her baby's future happiness.

"I get it," she said, letting her own arms drop and taking a step back. "It's cool if you're into that. I . . . I like you," she admitted. "I just can't base my whole future on someone who might up and leave when I'm not pregnant anymore."

He burst out laughing, capturing her arms, tugging her back against him. "I may be a pervert, sweetheart, but it doesn't have anything to do with that baby in your belly." He nuzzled her throat, pressed a kiss to the spot in between her collarbones. "It's you, baby. *You're* what makes me crazy. Not your body—though I do love that," he said, hands slipping down as he did some of his own squeezing on *her* great hockey ass. "It's what's in here"—he let go to lightly tap her temple—"and here"—the spot above her heart.

"That doesn't make sense," she argued. "It's not like we've gotten to know each other or spent loads of time alone together. There's always been a barrier between us because I'm on the coaching staff."

"I don't have to have spent time with you alone to see the person you are, Calle," he said.

She scoffed. "That's ridiculous."

"I know who you are because I've seen you at team events, how great you are with the kids, how you always make sure everyone is included. I've seen you be beyond patient with the media when they ask you the same damn questions every time. I've even seen you play, been so fucking impressed with your talent and athleticism." He tugged lightly on a lock of her hair. "I swear if you had two good knees and six more inches, you'd be giving Blue a run for his money for leading scorer in the league. And, I've seen you with the team—I've seen calm and steady Calle even under stressful circumstances—"

"I'm certainly not calm and steady Calle now," she said. "I've spent the last hour freaking out over what to wear and then the last ten minutes arguing with you."

"Baby." His lips dropped, halting just the barest distance from hers.

Immediately, her worries faded, and she was almost desperate to close the gap between their mouths, to get just one more kiss, to feel his body against hers.

"Maybe you're not your normal self," he said softly, his words coating her lips in damp heat. "Maybe you're on edge and feeling like the whole world changed in the blink of an eye—"

And yes, that was exactly how she felt. He knew it, too, based on the smile he gave her, the stink. "But your world *did* shift and change, and all your plans and thoughts for the future went alongside with it." She inhaled, ready to argue that it didn't matter, that was life, that she was still almost unhinged, but Coop finally closed the distance between their mouths and kissed the words out of her.

When he broke apart, his lightly calloused thumb was tracing her jaw. "Everything changed," he said. "And yet, you're right here where you should be. In my arms, arguing with me, yes, but not arguing in a way that's mean or hurtful and is more about you trying to get whatever fucked up shit is swirling in your head out of it." A beat. "And *I'm* here because I'm fucking crazy about you, and I want to help you get rid of that shit so you and I can make something incredible together. So . . . are you with me?"

He'd said a lot.

So much that her head was spinning, and she almost didn't know where to begin.

But then he dropped his arms and picked up her hand, lacing their fingers together before pressing a kiss to the backs of hers. "So, love, are you with me?"

A shuddering breath.

Yes, she was with him. God, she liked this man so. Fucking. Much. But she had to make sure, just as she was researching and double-checking and confirming everything about her pregnancy with her doctor and Devon and Becca, she also needed to make sure Coop would be looked out for.

She squeezed his hand. "You'll tell me at the first sign?"

That damned brow came up again. "Tell you what?"

"Promise me you'll tell me when you're done, when it's too much. I won't be hurt," she said, talking quickly and lying through her teeth because she knew that the moment she let Coop in, that he'd be *all* in, and as thus (also, fucking more *thuses* —she really needed to expand her vocabulary), but the point was, that when he did eventually leave, it was going to hurt like hell.

And what about her baby?

She felt a blip of panic about an innocent child getting attached to wonderful Coop. She couldn't let her baby get hurt, not—

His free hand came up, cupped her cheek. "What just went through your mind?"

"I—" She broke off, unable to say the words.

"Never mind, baby," he said. "I can tell it's bullshit."

"Coop."

"I'm not going anywhere."

"*Coop!*"

"Fucking *no*, baby. I get a shot at you, and I'm not just walking away. Absolutely not—"

She turned into him, cupped *his* cheek for a change. "Please, Coop."

His expression turned stony.

"Just promise me?"

Thunderclouds across dark eyes. "Fine. I fucking promise," he growled. "Okay. But also know that I'm not fucking leaving. Not now, not tomorrow, not *ever*."

She wished that would be true.

She *wanted* that to be true.

But that also wasn't her life.

"You don't believe me," he said, the statement quiet and flat, "do you?"

"I—"

Calle didn't want to hurt him, but she also didn't have the best track record with men—her father, her exes, with Jason being the biggest douche canoe of them all—and none of those relationships had the complications as did hers and Coops—their careers at odds and a baby that wasn't his on the way.

"Then I'll just have to prove it to you."

"Coop . . ."

He brushed his lips over her forehead then pulled back, and his face was filled with such softness and affection that she gave in to the inevitable. She'd been fending off her attraction to him for two long years, and all the while she'd gotten to know him better, seen glimpses of the sweet, protective, caring man underneath, and that made her resolve crumble away like a cookie dipped in tea.

She melted, softened.

Yes, she knew she was probably dooming herself to a broken heart.

But she was going for this time with Coop.

Because a man like him didn't come around but once in a lifetime. She opened her mouth to tell him that, to let him know she was giving in to the inevitable, that she was going to go along for the ride and not look back, but he didn't give her the chance.

Coop took her hand and led her out of her bedroom.

THIRTEEN

COOP

He'd placed the bag of takeout on her coffee table, a salad from Molly's for him and the grilled cheese he knew was her favorite for Calle. He'd also bought soup and tea, both seeming like the type of comfort food a pregnant woman would want. Of course, in probably stupid fashion, he'd asked Brit what Calle's favorites were.

Yes, talking to Brit might have been a mistake.

Just inquiring about her favorite foods from Molly's was going to have the gossip train leaving the station, chugging through the locker room as speculation went wild with what was going on between them. But Coop was also done with tiptoeing around. He'd begun with pushy and persistent, and he was going to see it through until he'd made his way through that tough outer layer Calle wore around her like a shield. Which was why he'd made some calls the night before, discussing the potential of him and Calle with Bernard and then PR-Rebecca.

After they'd given him the fifth degree, Bernard especially, Coop had discovered what Calle had meant when referencing her contract the day before.

Apparently, Bernard thought he was doing them both a solid by clearing the way with legal, HR, and the board. Coop still couldn't quite believe that his coach had been playing matchmaker, but he had, ensuring a clause was put in Calle's contract that protected her from any fallout from dating him. Bernard had also made it clear that if things continued the way they'd been going, and Coop's agent finalized the deal they were working on, that same clause would be included in his offer.

So, one crisis avoided.

The next was what the blogs and sports shows would say.

But PR-Rebecca was the shit. She'd handle whatever storm blew their way. Which meant that the only roadblock in his way with Calle was Calle herself.

And he didn't think he was wrong in knowing it would be the hardest to overcome.

Still, she'd agreed to give him a chance.

That was something.

Unpacking why she'd make him promise to tell her when his feelings began to change was a whole other issue.

One he was going to tackle on another day.

"I should change my clothes," she began to say. "Put on something that's not sweats—"

He snagged her hand when she turned back to the bedroom, tugging her over to the couch and the coffee table. "You don't need to change," he told her. "We're staying in."

"I—um—" A shake of her head that sent brown hair skidding over her shoulders. "That's probably not a good idea."

Coop thought it was the best idea he'd ever had, holding Calle captive so she couldn't avoid him. Being in her condo also had the side benefit of giving him the ability to kiss her whenever he felt like it.

Though, holding her captive probably wasn't the best term.

Either way, he'd shown up for their date, had found the door unlocked, and had made his way inside, and since they'd been on their own for a good half hour now and no police had shown up because a scary black dude had entered a white woman's condo, Coop figured they were safe from busybody neighbors.

Though, now he needed to have a conversation with her about locking her doors.

Figuring that would probably go over as well as him suggesting they date in the first place, he decided to put that conversation off for the moment and focus on plying Calle with carbs.

He pulled out her sandwich and handed it to her, along with a cup of whatever magical homemade soup Molly had put together.

"Eat," he said, shoving them at her.

Since the soup had bacon and a shit ton of cream and cheese in it, Coop had satisfied himself with only a smell.

It definitely wasn't on the diet plan.

And his torture at passing over the soup without taking a taste seemed to make Calle relax when nothing else could.

"It's killing you to not eat this, isn't it?" she asked, scooping up a large mouthful.

Her moan, when the spoon slid between her lips, made his cock harden. Just like that, just that easy, skipped right over chub and went directly to granite.

God damn.

"You're evil."

She smirked and took another bite. "I've never been so glad to not be a player any longer than when I realized I didn't have to follow that food plan." She set down the soup and picked up her sandwich, taking a huge bite. "Don't get me wrong, Rebecca does an amazing job and I know it's working. I'm . . ."

"Just glad you can eat whatever you want?"

"That." Her lips twitched. "Well, with the exception of alcohol and more than one cup of coffee and ibuprofen and—"

Her sandwich was there, right there, just a few inches from his face and teasing him.

So. Not. Fair.

He bent and took a nibble.

Just one bite wouldn't gain Nutritionist-Rebecca's notice, right?

Hell, who was he kidding? She'd take one look and know exactly what he'd done wrong. But Coop found he couldn't summon a damn to give, not when Calle gasped and snatched the sandwich back then nearly toppled off the couch. He lurched forward and snagged her around the waist while she fought to keep the sandwich away from him. He was pretending to gnaw at her arm, teeth snapping at the grilled cheese, as giggles exploded from her chest.

Those giggles were the best thing he'd ever heard.

They were a hundred times better than the crowd cheering when he scored, even better than hearing his name called when he'd been drafted.

Because they were pure Calle.

And that meant they were solid gold.

At the end of their struggle, they ended up in a heap on the carpet, Calle sprawled across his chest, the nibbled-on sandwich still gripped in her hand. "I win," she said proudly, lifting it up like she was hefting the Cup.

Coop took advantage of her distraction and shot up to sitting, hands coming to her waist to keep her in place as he dropped his mouth to hers.

"No," he said when he pulled away. "I'm the one who's won, sweetheart."

Or at least the first battle, anyway.

———

Operation Out-Stubborn continued the next day when he waited until Calle was seated in the back of the plane, fully buckled in at the window seat. Excellent (cue Mr. Burns fingers here). Coop got up, walked down the aisle and seated himself directly next to her.

"I have some questions," he said, fighting a grin and totally failing.

Because . . . fuck, he just liked being around her.

He'd stayed later than he should have the night before, considering the travel day they both had and the extra rest she should be getting.

Coop had plowed through one pregnancy book to learn that.

And had six others on his kindle.

Fuck, pregnancy seemed like a shitty hand to be dealt— nausea, vomiting, no alcohol, shit she couldn't eat, and then at the end of it, Calle got to push an eight-pound watermelon-shaped object out of her—

"What the fuck are you doing?" she hissed.

"Sitting with the woman I'm in a relationship with," he said, nonplussed.

"We're not—" Her mouth opened and closed a few times. "A relationship— No, that's not—"

"Last night, you were in my arms and agreed to give us a shot. Did you change your mind?"

Her gaze dropped to her hands and for the first time since he'd started down this path, Coop felt a bolt of fear. *Had* she changed her mind? Fuck that, he wasn't going to let her change her mind —no fucking way.

Chocolate eyes drifted back up to his. "No," she whispered.

Everything in him settled, and Coop knew his plan was working. He had to keep moving forward, keep pressing until he was so ingrained inside her that she wouldn't be able to picture a world without him.

"Good," he said, leaning down and brushing his lips over hers.

Which meant that instantly the cabin of the plane was filled with chattering, the gossip train chugging right along as those who could see them were informing those who couldn't that he'd just kissed Calle.

In front of everyone.

Coop figured it was easier that way.

Everyone now knew and they could move on, not having to hide behind curtains or in the showers, al la Gabe and Nutritionist Rebecca and Stefan and Brit, respectively.

He loved Calle, no way was he hiding it.

He. *Loved*. Calle.

A bolt of shock hit him in the gut before he settled. Because, *of course*, he loved Calle. If he didn't, would he have gone through all of this trouble? Would he have pushed and pressed and been obsessed with anyone less than the woman he loved?

Fuck, no.

Coop didn't court trouble.

But he sure as shit was going to court Calle.

Until she fell in love with him right back.

FOURTEEN

CALLE

She glanced up at the knock on the door then down at herself. It was late and she was cramming in a few more hours, trying to lock down the system and any plays that needed tweaking before the next day's game.

So, in her pajamas printed with sheep and her baggy hoodie, she wasn't exactly dressed to impress.

Setting her notebook aside, she stood and crossed to the door.

Then was disappointed when it wasn't Coop on the other side of the door.

"Stupid," she muttered. They'd gone their separate ways after grabbing dinner that evening in the hotel restaurant, him to rest up, her . . . well, she'd said she was going to rest up, but it had been a lie as she'd known she was going to come up and work.

She just hadn't wanted to get into a discussion about it.

Not when they'd had a nice conclusion to the night before, and not when the dinner had been filled with laughter and joking. It was so easy to spend time with Coop, and she'd wanted to hold on to that, not prick his protective streak and get into an argument with him.

"He probably wouldn't argue," she muttered, seeing the tray in the worker's hand outside the door and beginning to unlock the dead bolt.

She needed to tell him she hadn't ordered—

Tugging the handle down, she pulled the panel open, lips parting to tell him he had the wrong room.

But before she could form words, the hotel employee extended a note.

Then nudged her to the side and brought the tray in, setting it on the desk next to her work as she tore the note open.

Because I know you're working and at least you can fuel up.
-C

She folded the paper, turning to frown at the desk and the tray and the employee. Then she blinked and realized she probably needed to tip the man. But when she reached for her purse, he shook his head, told her it had been taken care of, then nudged her back to the side and disappeared into the hall, closing the door with a decisive *click*.

Her cell buzzed, and she extracted it from the pocket of her hoodie.

Coop had texted.

Did you lock up?

She sighed, but her lips were twitching.

It was one time.

A beat then,

So, you locked up?

Calle shook her head, flipped the dead bolt closed along with the lock, and then typed back.

Yes.

Good.

She nibbled on her bottom lip as she made her way over to the desk and felt her heart pulse when she saw the fruit salad.

Then her cheeks creased when she spied the slice of carrot cake.

Her favorite.

Can't figure out how you think a vegetable is dessert, but enjoy.

Heart swelling, she replied.

I'm surprised you didn't send me a cheesecake so you could live vicariously through me.

A buzz.

I was tempted.

She plucked up a strawberry and bit into the juicy goodness on a moan.

I wish I was there to lick the taste of what you were eating right off your lips.

Calle froze, heat arrowing for her center.

Add in that thing you did with your fingers last time and I'd let you.

Silence for a long moment.

Next hotel, I'm finding a way to sneak into your room.

Why not sneak up now?

She found herself texting, even though it was late, even though there was a game tomorrow. Desperation was a powerful motivator, especially when Coop had played her body like a violin every single time they were together.

Bernard's got the room at the end of the hall and I swear to God he gave me a look when I came back to mine.

Her mouth quirked up.

What kind of look?

A buzz.

The kind that said he'd kill me if I even thought of walking down the hall to your room. It was the quintessential 'dad look.'

She hesitated then,

A 'dad look?'

Definitely a 'dad look.' Bernard's got a soft spot for you.

Calle scoffed.

Not sure about that.

Well, my balls are quite sure about that. Despite being very

*blue from wanting you, they're also very scared because they
don't want Bernard removing them from my body. So, let's
agree to disagree and call it very strong 'dad vibes'.*

She felt a curl of pleasure at the notion, especially when it
filled a hole inside her, one that had remained open and gaping
after her father had left.
Another buzz.

*Very scary 'dad vibes.' But it's good you have someone
looking after you.*

She was just starting to realize how many people were really
looking after her. Coop. Bernard. PR Rebecca. Stefan and Brit.
The rest of the guys on the team. But really, it all circled back to
Coop looking after her. Because he was the one who made her
heart feel as though it were pumped full of helium. Especially
when his next text said,

*You shouldn't work too late. The book said that you still
need lots of sleep.*

Looking after her. Presumably reading baby books.
That should be terrifying, but instead, she wanted more.
Dangerous thinking, dangerous notions, dangerous feelings.
But that still didn't stop her from texting.

If you'd knocked, I would have opened the door.

And it didn't stop her from grinning when he replied with,

Absolutely killing me, sweetheart.

———

Two nights later, she shook out her hands, semi-frozen from standing behind on the bench. No matter that she'd spent countless seasons in this position actually sitting on the bench where the players rested between shifts, Calle could never get her bare hands used to the cold.

Hockey gloves, no problem.

Bare skin, painful and tingly.

It was a couple of minutes until puck drop and the Gold were filing out onto the ice, Brit leading the way. Coop was bringing up the rear, and she knew why when he stopped briefly by her, nudging her shoulder with his and lightly patting her belly before he strode out of the hall into view of the cameras and fans.

A little forward, that touch to her belly.

But she didn't hate it.

In fact, it gave her that helium feeling again. Biting her lip, so fucking into this man, Calle almost didn't realize he'd stopped at the mouth of the hall.

She lifted her brows in question.

He gestured to her waist.

Frowning, she glanced down, but didn't see anything awry and looked back up, shrugging. He was too far away for her to hear his sigh, but she knew he had anyway. But then he lifted his arms to the side and mimed . . .

Oh.

He mimed putting his hands in pockets before gesturing at her to do the same.

"What the—" She began but then her hands were in her pockets . . . and they were toasty warm. He'd slipped her hand warmers without her knowing. More care. More watching out for her.

Helium.

Hope.

Her eyes lifted, but he'd already gone through, and she was alone in the hallway with toasty warm hands.

Although, was she really alone when she had a man like Coop in her corner?

———

Peanut butter M&Ms in her laptop bag.

She pulled out the red bag with a shake of her head.

Coop had gone out to dinner with Brit, Stefan, and Max, but she'd stayed in, tired after a late night of travel and the press she'd done today.

And he was still taking care of her.

Shaking her head, Calle crawled into bed, taking her cell and the bag of candy with her.

How'd you know?

He replied to her text in seconds. Which was probably rude because he was out to dinner with friends, but she was selfish enough to be happy that he'd responded so quickly.

More danger.

But she was ignoring the internal warning and focusing on how good it felt to be the center of Coop's universe.

Even if being that center might not last.

I'd have to have been an idiot to miss your shrine to peanut butter at your place.

Okay, so maybe she'd gone a bit overboard in her pregnancy stash buying, but fuck, if the baby didn't enjoy peanut butter, too.

It had been the only thing she hadn't puked up during those miserable weeks.

You're observant.

A buzz.

It's not a big deal.

Her response was rapid.

It is to me.

His response came just as quickly.

I'm glad, but also, it's not hard to discover what your woman likes if you're paying attention. Anyone who doesn't is a douchebag.

Well, apparently, she'd only ever dated douchebags. But then again, she already knew that, didn't she?

So, you haven't kissed me in a while.

A beat.

Technically you haven't kissed ME in a while either.

She smiled.

Come to my room when you get back, and I'll get on it.

Can't. Bernard's still playing chaperone.

sad face Not even for a goodnight kiss?

two sad faces I like my balls where they are, and I think you'll feel the same if you really think about it.

Calle sighed and then yawned.

Fine. Well, then, I'm going to bed. Goodnight.

Rest up, love.

Love.

Her heart skipped a beat, but then she opened her tablet, intending to put on an old episode of SVU to fall asleep to when she saw it.

It being the stat-tracking app she'd mentioned in passing, the one she'd been waffling about ordering because it had an annual membership fee of ninety-nine dollars and ninety-nine cents, and that was about ninety-eight dollars more than she'd ever spent on any app.

She clicked the icon and immediately fell in love.

It was everything she'd wanted, ticked all of the boxes for things she'd dreamed about.

Instantly in love.

Only, she didn't think she was talking about the app at all.

FIFTEEN

COOP

"Psst!" Max hissed.

Coop looked up from his stall, and his teammate gave him a nod.

"Thanks," he mouthed, knowing he'd owe him one.

Operation Out-Stubborn had transformed into Operation Woo and because his team were a bunch of nosy assholes—and also really cool—they were on his side. Well, that and Calle had apparently told Mandy who'd told Brit about the carrot cake and the peanut butter M&Ms and the app and . . . well, the jig had been up when he'd sat next to her on the plane, but now it was really up.

The side benefit was that now he had backup.

Of the Brit, Stefan, Mike, Max, Mandy, and the dual-Rebeccas sort. And that didn't even count the head trainer, Gabe, telling him to "Keep at it, because it's worth it in the end" or Blue's fist bump when he saw Coop delivering a peanut-butter slathered bagel to Calle's office that morning.

Whatever the title, his plan was working.

Calle had opened the door a sliver, and he was working on

nudging it just a millimeter wider at a time until he had full access.

And the team was helping.

Max included.

Calle was currently on the other side of the room, talking to Blue while Max accomplished his task. Mostly because when she'd walked into the room, she'd pointed a finger at Coop and told him to behave.

Which made the room at large cackle.

Because they'd all seen the giant jar of peanut butter he'd bought and left outside her office door before the game. Mostly because they'd had to walk by it—a jaunty red bow wrapped around its lid—to get to the ice.

"How am I supposed to get that home?" she'd asked, stopping two feet inside the room, hands plunking onto her hips as she glared at him.

"I figured you'd finish it before the next plane ride."

Narrowed eyes, upturned lips, and then finally . . . *finally* she met him in the middle. Well, the *side*, anyway. She'd crossed the space and laid a kiss on him that had the whole room catcalling before she released him and calmly walked to the other side of the space, as though she regularly kissed him in front of a gaggle of hockey players.

After his pulse had settled, he'd glanced at Max.

His friend was already prepped and had slipped out to leave just one more thing outside her office.

The perfect complement to the peanut butter . . . or at least that was what she'd tried to convince him of the night before— that there was no snack more perfect than peanut butter and apples.

So, he gave her both.

He couldn't wait to see her reaction.

Slowly, she made her rounds with the offense as everyone removed their equipment and took their turns in the shower. She checked in with everyone except for him. Or rather, she left him for last, he realized, when she came to sit next to him, iPad in hand.

They went through a few clips Dani, the video coach, had pulled and then her face got soft and she cupped his cheek. "You're too sweet," she murmured.

He held her eyes. "You deserve sweet."

She slowly inhaled. "I'm starting to believe that." Her eyes flicked around the space. Most of the team had already finished changing and were heading off to complete their post-game routines, so the space was mostly empty. "Thank you."

He shook his head. "What could you possibly be thanking me for?"

"I don't know." She pushed to her feet. "Maybe the peanut butter or the candy or the cake?"

"You're not thanking me for the cake," he said.

Her face was way too serious for something as simple as a thank you for a piece of cake or a jar of peanut butter, even a really big one.

A sigh. "No, I'm not. It's—" She faltered for a moment, but he gave her that moment, somehow instinctively knowing that what she was going to tell him was big, something that would make a lot of the pieces come together.

So, he waited, put pushy to the side for the moment.

He gave her that time.

And what she told him made him glad he did it.

"I know we've had this weird mix of intimacy and barely knowing each other," she said hurriedly. "When you said you'd spent the last two years getting to know me even though I purposely made sure to keep my distance, I realized that you were right. Being on a team like this, being in close quarters, our lives were bound to overlap in some ways. It was stupid of me to think they wouldn't, after spending a lifetime on teams, after experiencing that overlap time and again. It was really fucking too stupid to think that just because I was pretending to be indifferent, I actually was."

A breath.

"That overlap is the same reason I know Max is obsessed with *Skylanders* and that Brit loves all boy bands, including for some godawful reason, Hansen." Her lips curved, but then her eyes went serious. "It's why I know Brayden"—Max's son—"just changed his favorite color to rainbow and that Mandy and Blane's daughter is teething and not sleeping well." She touched his chest lightly. "It's also why I know you, Coop. Why I know about your clean car and your obsession for all things cheese. But it's more than that, too. Because I also know you always felt a little like an outsider, not because the older guys deliberately left you out, but because you're younger, yet an old soul and so don't really connect well to younger, single guys or the older ones with families."

Coop's throat was tight and fuck him, his eyes actually stung.

He knew *he'd* been paying attention, but he hadn't realized that Calle had also been doing the same. Even though she'd been hurt by that asshole Jason, even though something about her past that she hadn't felt safe enough to share had scarred her, she'd still been paying attention.

"I know that, because growing up, I felt the same. Like I didn't belong at home"—her expression went sad—"but hockey gave me the space to find my niche . . . and it led me to you. And I'm so damned scared all the time, scared that you'll weave yourself so deeply into my life and then leave, a-and I'm terrified that you want me now, but that one day you're going to wake up and realize that it's not me you want—" She broke off, chest rising and falling, tears slipping from the corners of her eyes. "And I don't want you to ever feel trapped."

Coop was quiet for a long moment, waiting in case she needed to say more, but when she didn't, he carefully wove his arms around her and tugged her into his lap. Brushing back the hair on her face, he asked, "Why would I feel trapped?"

No answer, aside from a long sniff, a hand dashing away tears.

"Baby, I'm the one who's pushed for this."

Her chin dropped to her chest, but then she inhaled and exhaled deeply. "So did my dad."

"What?"

"My dad pursued my mom, pursued her until she finally gave in and then he resented her when she got pregnant." She made a face. "Unfortunately, not enough to leave. Instead, he married her, made two more kids in quick succession, and then set about making our lives miserable."

Aw, fuck. "Baby."

"He was a miserable son of a bitch, but my mom was great, even though it was fucking painful to see her happiness chipped away by him over the years. She tried so hard and . . . nothing she ever did or said mattered."

His heart fucking ached, but he couldn't take away her pain, couldn't make the past not happen. He could, however, listen.

"I think I always knew I was the reason for his unhappiness," she said quietly. "I think that's why I tried so hard. His favorite sport was hockey and I vowed to be the best player there was." She shrugged, mouth turned up in a rueful smile. "Clearly, that didn't happen, but I was at least able to eventually put that all aside and achieve my own goals, to find my love for the game. But it wasn't just hockey, I spent my whole childhood being like my mom, trying to please him, desperate for him to be proud and—" A tear slipped out. "He wasn't able to be that person for me."

Fury was whipping through him as he wiped the glistening drop away.

"What he was, was a fucking asshole," Coop snapped then had to force himself to calm his tone. "You figured out how to be a good person for yourself, baby. You did it without him. Made your own way, and you're really fucking incredible for doing it."

"I'm just—"

"Insanely smart? Kind? Sassy in a way that makes me want to kiss the sharpness right out of your words and taste that tartness on my tongue?"

Her head started to shake.

He gave in to what he'd been resisting for long moments.

Coop kissed the woman he loved. He kissed her until she melted against him. He kissed her so thoroughly that he barely noticed Richie coming in to collect the discarded equipment, barely heard Brit's broken-off exclamation when she strode back into the room then quickly left.

He could kiss Calle through a hurricane, through a sand-storm, through a—

She pushed lightly at his chest and he lifted his head, stroking his thumb lightly over her lips.

"Why today?" he asked. "Why tell me all of this today?"

Her brows drew together in question. "What?"

"I guess I'm asking . . . what changed? Why aren't you scared anymore?"

He'd been expecting a long, drawn-out courtship, winning her over by millimeters, but today she'd just nonchalantly opened the door wide.

"Oh, I'm more scared than I've ever been in my life." She lifted a finger when he started to reply, a reply he bit back because she smiled up at him, eyes reddened from tears, but so warm that he felt that warmth soak into him.

She was more beautiful in that moment than he'd ever seen her, and words simply wouldn't come.

Hers were better anyway.

Especially when she leaned in, so their lips were almost touching. "Because of that stupid jar of peanut butter. I looked at it, at the red bow, and realized that you're nothing like my dad. He might have pursued my mom, but he never *ever* took the time to really get to know her." She brushed her lips over his. "He didn't even know her favorite color after having been married for twenty-six years."

"That's . . . "

"Classic asshole, which my dad perfected."

Yeah, he seemed to have done that one thing—and only that

thing—really well. Fuck, to think the man missed out on the absolute wonderfulness that was Calle.

Idiot.

"What are you thinking?" she asked, fingers running lightly up and down the outside of his arms. She hadn't made to move off his lap and he wasn't ready to let her go, not when she felt so good there.

So, he told her. "That your dad is a fucking asshole."

Chuckles against his lips then drifting through the fabric of his shirt, soaking into his skin when she rested her forehead on his shoulder.

"You're right."

He threaded his fingers in her ponytail and gently lifted her head. "Where are they now?"

"Both gone," she said, eyes sad. "Mom to cancer and my dad just kind of faded away afterward. My sister lives in New York, and my brother moved to Germany with his partner."

"You're on the West Coast all alone."

"Yes." She stood up and reached for his hand, squeezing it lightly. "Only today, I realized that I *wasn't* alone." She stared into his eyes, telling him without words that *he'd* made her feel that way.

"Baby."

Then she gave him the words.

"Because I realized that I had *you*." His heart pulsed when she squeezed again.

"Calle."

"I love you, Coop."

"Baby."

She smiled. "I made a decision when I saw that silly jar of peanut butter in the hall. I realized I had a man who knew me, who cared enough about me to discover all the little details about the things I prefer. The one who took me to my doctor's appointment and got teary-eyed when he heard my baby's heartbeat when he wasn't even the father." Her hand lifted to his jaw. "So, I decided I was going to stop being afraid. I decided I was going to keep you and pray that you'd want to keep me, too."

"Cal—"

She opened her mouth, and he decided he'd had enough words.

Coop tugged her against his chest, banding his arms around her and holding her tight. "I'm really pissed . . . you beat me to saying 'I love you,' first."

Her expression had clouded when he'd begun the sentence.

By the end, she was grinning up at him. Then she buffed her knuckles on her chest. "You know what they say about being first," she teased. "That second place is just the first loser."

He snorted.

"Well, I'm happy to lose to you, sweetheart." He bent so their lips were close again. "Especially if it means that I get to kiss you whenever I want."

She wound her arms around his neck. "I can live with that."

Coop closed the distance between their mouths and took her at her word.

Sixteen

Calle

Truth be told, she managed to make more than a dent in that jar of peanut butter before she boarded the return flight home.

Also, the truth had come out.

The team knew she and Coop were together, along with the board and the rest of the coaching staff . . . and the media.

But luckily for her, Brit and Stefan had paved the way and while there were plenty of opinions shared on the hockey blogs, the coverage had been minimal and their "love affair" had been quickly eclipsed by the unexpected divorce of a famous A-list couple.

In the locker room and on the ice, however, the chirps hadn't disappeared quite so quickly.

The team teased each other relentlessly on any given day and she and Coop were providing plenty of new material, especially because the gifts hadn't stopped.

The bushel of apples placed outside the office she'd been using for the away game by Max when she'd been distracted and after which she'd consumed all five pounds of them . . . along with the peanut butter.

Then when she got back to her condo after the road trip, a courier had brought her a copy of a book she was looking for, one that didn't come in eBook and could only be special ordered. A book she'd mentioned barely in passing.

Then more treats over the last two days.

The man just didn't stop.

Not that she wanted him to.

Especially because tonight they were going on a date. A real one that she was going to get dressed for because she'd ordered some maternity clothes online and they didn't look too bad—especially the jeans and sparkly tank top that gave her serious cleavage

The puking had stopped.

Her boobage had increased.

The man was getting lucky.

He'd more than earned it, and she'd found that, along with having boobs that touched for the first time in her life, her sex drive was off the charts.

Maybe it was pregnancy hormones.

Maybe it was Coop.

Hell, who was she kidding. It was most definitely Coop.

Calle pulled up the jeans, glad the elastic on the waist meant she could easily button them, and then slipped into the tank top. A brush through her hair, a quick smoky eye a teammate had taught her long ago, and a glance down to ensure her new boobs had the proper amount of containment—that being not too much as to inadvertently flash everyone in the vicinity, but enough that Coop's eyes would bug out of his head when he saw her.

The doorbell rang, and she hurried to answer it.

Coop was on the other side.

His eyes bugged.

She grinned, heart rolling over in her chest. "See?" she said. "I'm remembering to lock my doors nowadays."

He crowded into her, pulling her into his arms and then bending to press his lips to hers, kissing her without preamble. She was really glad she hadn't bothered with lipstick. It would have been a mess—

His tongue slid inside her mouth, dancing with hers and just like that, she was ready.

She tugged him, trying to wrestle the man who outweighed her by a good forty pounds through her door with all of the success as someone attempting to wrestle an elephant.

Or maybe a camel.

Or—

He lifted his head. "Is there a problem?"

Her chest rose and fell rapidly. "No. I want you inside. Now," she added when another tug didn't move him.

A flash of white, lips she really loved kissing turning up at the edges.

"We're going to dinner," he reminded her.

"Not anymore," she declared . . . and yes, it was a declaration. An imperious one at that.

"Calle—"

"Coop," she said. "We have a night off. We're together. There aren't any teammates to come barging through the door, and we don't have a game tonight or practice tomorrow. We have twenty-four hours, and I want to spend them just with you."

"But you got dressed up—"

Another tug and this time he let her pull him through the front door. "I got dressed up for you, silly man. Because I wanted you to take one look at me and get hard. Because I've been dreaming about you kissing more than my lips, and I can't go another night without knowing how you feel inside me."

Silence.

Then he peeled her hand away from his.

Her heart sank.

He brought her palm down and settled it over his pelvis—correction, he settled it over the hard jut of his erection and when her fingers instinctively closed over it, he groaned and thrust into her hand, growling, "Baby."

"Coop," she murmured, leaning in to kiss the base of his throat. God, she loved that spot.

"Baby."

Her eyes lifted to his.

"You sure?"

"Yes." No hesitation. No waffling. No more wasting time on the past when she needed to enjoy the present.

To enjoy Coop.

He moved before the thought cleared her mind, scooping her up into his arms as though she weighed absolutely nothing.

Then they were moving down the hall and into the bedroom.

Then she was flat on her back with Coop sprawled out on top of her.

"Sure?" he asked again.

She propped her elbows beneath her and nipped his chin. "I already said I was sure."

"Sass." He grinned. "I love it." He leaned back, reaching for the hem of her top and inching under it, lightly stroking his fingers, back and forth, back and forth. Goose bumps lifted on her skin, her nerves prickled with awareness, and she was desperate for his hands to move—either up or down. In that instant, she didn't care.

But then he bent and nipped *her* chin. "And I love you."

God, she didn't think she'd ever get tired of hearing those words emerge from his lips.

Though, in that moment, she'd prefer if they'd emerge when he was naked.

He seemed to read that thought as it ran across her mind. "I'm trying to go slow here, love. Make sure—"

She batted his hands away and grabbed the hem of her shirt, yanking it up and over her head, tossing it to the side without bothering to see where it landed. Coop's eyes did that thing again, not really bugging so much as slightly widening and then sparking to life with heat that threatened to scorch her skin.

Oh. She should have probably also mentioned that she'd invested in lingerie.

Silky, lacy, see-through lingerie.

Which Coop apparently enjoyed, because he unleashed a string of curse words that impressed even her, and she didn't think there were words like that which she *hadn't* heard.

"Slow, next time," he growled.

She nodded. "I agree."

One movement had her pants off. The next had his shirt. The one after that *his* pants.

And—for real—his body was insane.

Flat abs that bore the hint of a six-pack even as he was leaning over her, pecs that were perfectly grab-able, cut biceps and triceps, forearms that made her wonder how often he'd worked his stick off the ice—

Heh.

"What went through your mind?" he asked, slipping a hand behind her back and undoing the clasp of her bra.

She told him.

He burst out laughing and then slanted his mouth across hers, all while laughing, so she felt his amusement deep inside her soul. "Fuck, if that ain't the truth," he said when he'd pulled away, fingers still resting against the skin of her back. "I've made myself come so many times over the past two years, it's not even funny." He pressed a kiss to her temple, her jaw. "And it was your face, your body I imagined every time."

He straightened, peeling off her bra and tossing it to the side. Then tugged her panties down her hips and off her feet.

She bit her lip.

Coop's expression went gentle. "What?" he asked.

A shake of her head. "It's nothing. I—" She didn't want to admit that she was a little self-conscious with the weight gain.

That was fucking stupid—and plus, boobs!—but a part of her wished he could have seen her when her body was—

Mouth on hers, tongue sliding deep, hands molding to her newfound curves.

"You are, without out a doubt, the most beautiful woman I've ever been with," he said, staring deep into her eyes. "Ever."

"I—"

"*Ever.*" A beat as he thrust forward, his hard cock rubbing between her thighs and making her gasp. "Now stop arguing with me. I'm on a mission to give my woman orgasms."

Did he say—?

He lifted a palm, cupped her breast, and his eyes heated further.

Yup. He'd said *orgasms.* As in plural.

And when he slid down her body to take the sensitive bud of one nipple into his mouth, fingers slipping between her thighs, instantly finding her clit and settling into a rhythm that had her catapulting up the edge, she knew he'd make good on his promise.

He switched breasts, rolling her other nipple between thumb and forefinger.

That, paired with the circling pressure on her clit, already had her scarily close to the edge.

"Coop!" she gasped when he nipped the underside of her breast, but then his mouth was sliding down, his fingers continuing their dance. Only then, his tongue joined the mix.

And that was it.

One flick of it against her clit, one finger slipping inside . . . and she exploded, his name on her lips. He saw her through the peak, licking and sucking and coaxing her down the other side.

Lazily, she slit her lids open.

Coop was poised over her, eyes molten, jaw hard . . . so fucking beautiful it took her breath away.

He reached to the side, grabbed his pants, and extracted a condom.

She smiled, murmured, "Don't think you need that, baby."

His eyes shot to hers. "I can't get more pregnant."

"You can still get diseases." he said, voice rasping.

"I'm clean," she said, propping herself up on her elbows again. "And I'm guessing you know your status since the team regularly tests everyone."

His eyes dropped to her breasts and she had to say, she liked those things.

"I'm clean, too," he said, hands rubbing up and down her sides. "But the last test was three months ago."

"Have you slept with anyone else since then?"

"No—"

She reached for his cock, tugging it free of the material of his boxer briefs. "Well then. Inside, please."

"Cal—"

Lifting her hips, she brushed her wet pussy against him.

And that was it.

The leash snapped.

Coop became a flurry of movement, body dropping to hers, her hand trapped between them, still wrapped around his cock, as he kissed and stroked and teased every part of her that he could reach. One moment his mouth was on hers, then he was sucking deeply at her nipples then he was nipping at her collarbone, her jaw, her throat.

Moisture pooled between her legs.

Desire made her vision hazy.

Need made her limbs shake.

Coop's cock pulsing in her hand made her realize she could solve both their problems. A shift of her waist, an angling of her hips and—

Fucking nirvana.

He was big, stretching her as just the head slipped inside then stretching her more when he groaned and thrust deep.

"Baby," he growled, nipping at her jaw. "I was trying—"

She turned and nipped *his* jaw. "Shut up and fuck me."

He shut up.

He fucked her.

Hard and deep and fast, he pounded into her, quickly winding her higher and higher and higher until she hovered just on the edge once more. Then he slowed. Then he paused. Her lips parted on a protest, breaths coming in sharp gasps.

"I love you."

Tears. As in, the way he said that, how he held himself frozen in place, his cock seated deep, his gaze intense, made tears fill her eyes.

She lifted her head and he got the message, kissing her again, then kissing away the tears when they escaped.

"And I'm not leaving," he growled, pulling out and thrusting back in.

She nodded. "I know."

"Never." Another thrust—one that took her dangerously close to the edge and left her moaning. "Never. Gonna. Leave. You. Calle."

More delicious movement. More moaning on her part.

But she did manage to gasp out, "I know, honey."

It was enough because his lips found hers, his rumbled, "Good," vibrating through her, and this time, he didn't stop until she tumbled over the edge, until with three more strokes he followed directly behind her.

She didn't hit dirt though.

Instead, Coop took her into his arms and held her as they both slowly wound their way down. And when she emerged from the haze of pleasure, she knew he'd made it his job to always be there to do the same.

"I love you," she murmured, letting her eyes slide closed.

Because for the first time in her life, she felt safe in a man's arms.

And she was planning on staying there.

———

"Oh my God!" Mandy shrieked and threw her arms around Calle a week later. "You're pregnant! That's amazing!"

Calle smiled, hugging her back, before retreating to sit on the edge of the table.

"Can I?" Mandy shook her head, stopping herself from reaching out. "I'm sorry, I always hated when people touched my belly without permission."

Calle laughed, taking Mandy's hand and placing it on her abdomen.

Those eight pounds had turned into a tiny baby bump to go along with her larger boobs.

She'd already decided she liked the bump better.

The boobs were annoying.

Her sports bras didn't fit, they kept getting in the way, and Coop couldn't keep his hands off them.

Though, in fairness, that last one wasn't the annoying part.

Mandy sighed. "Baby bumps are the best." She glanced down in the direction of her own abdomen. "Though I wish the whole bump thing would go away after the baby comes. My stomach will never be the same."

An arm slipped around Mandy's waist and Blane tugged her back against his chest. "I happen to like you just the way you are."

"Just like?" Mandy pouted.

He grinned and kissed her temple. "Why are you talking about your beautiful, gorgeously sexy body with my coach?"

"Because that one's"—Mandy pointed at Calle—"body is about to be ruined, too."

"Gee, thanks," Calle muttered.

Blane glanced at her, jaw dropping open.

"Also, seriously, you don't have to sound so gleeful about it," Calle continued her muttering, holding her breath as she waited for Blane's reaction. There was a reason she'd chosen to tell Mandy—knowing it would subsequently get to Blane—at this moment. The PT Suite was empty, and Mandy was nice.

She wouldn't judge.

Calle wasn't sure Blane would be the same.

"I have to be gleeful," Mandy cried. "Have you seen Monique?"—a former model and the wife of their former goalie —"she looked better after she had Mirabel than before. She's a freak of nature, and I'm not going to ever have a flat—"

Blane kissed her.

Calle had to give Coop props for picking up that habit. It was effective in cutting off meaningless rants.

"You're beautiful," he said, pulling back. "And you"—he turned to Calle—"Congrats to you and Coop."

"Oh," she began, "it's not actually—"

A hand dropped around her shoulders, a mouth pressed to hers, cutting her off.

Hmm.

Maybe taking away those props.

But then Coop gave her a taste of his delicious tongue, and Calle forgot to be annoyed.

"I agree with Blane," he said to Mandy after he'd broken the kiss. "You're absolutely beautiful." His eyes met Blane's. "And thanks, man."

She blinked.

Was he just going to pretend the baby was his?

Her confusion must have shown on her face because he bent and whispered in her ear. "DNA doesn't matter, sweetheart. This baby has been mine since that first appointment. And when I say I'm not leaving, I mean *I'm not leaving*." A kiss to her temple. "You or the baby. You get me?"

Heart rolling over in her chest, she nodded. "I get you."

"Good." He gave her a smile that sent her pulse sky high. The last time he'd worn it, his face had been between her thighs and he'd just made her come with his tongue. "Let's get you to your appointment." He held out a hand, helped her down from the table, then whispered in her ear again. "Because after that, I'm getting you home so that I can figure out what just went through your head."

Unable to stop herself, she rose on tiptoe, put her mouth to *his* ear, and told him.

His fingers spasmed on her hips.

His groan was barely audible.

Then he grinned again.

And she knew he'd make good on another of his promises.

————

"No, I couldn't," she said, a week later.

Coop held out the other half of his sandwich—her favorite grilled cheese from Sam and Cheese—because they'd stopped at the food stand that evening after her twenty-week ultrasound and picked up food to go. Everything looked good, though they'd need to get a repeat image in a few weeks because the placenta appeared to be growing a little lower than ideal. And since the baby hadn't cooperated and they hadn't been able to tell the gender, Calle was looking forward to another ultrasound to hopefully find out.

And another chance for her to watch Coop's face as he stared at the screen.

Another chance for her heart to expand.

"Your expression says differently," he said, pressing a kiss to her forehead and handing over the other half to his sandwich. She took it, because she really *was* ravenous and, aside from the eight-pound gain a month ago, she hadn't gained more in the time since. Dr. Holdings said that while she shouldn't go crazy, she shouldn't worry, that sometimes women gain in peaks and valleys.

"Thanks," she said around the bite of deliciousness.

"I'm ready for dessert, anyway," he told her and frowned, leaning back into her couch and picking up his cell. "I'll Door-Dash something. We should have picked up something at the outdoor market."

She snagged his cell from him, a call from his mom the reason she'd been able to sneak the brown bag back to her condo, and handed it over.

She'd bought him more brownies. More *cheesecake-swirled* brownies.

Because he needed her to know the little things, too.

That she'd been taking the time to pay attention.

His favorite color was turquoise. He loved cheese. He had a sweet tooth. He was obsessed with a certain brand of cinnamon gum. He . . . listened to historical romance audiobooks on his phone.

Yeah.

That one had shocked her, too, when she'd accidentally stumbled upon the secret on their most recent plane ride.

Coop had fallen asleep mid-flight from Chicago. She'd reached to pause his podcast—or what he'd told her he was listening to—so he wouldn't lose his place, and she'd discovered his deep, dark secret.

A secret she was now sworn to keep, under the pain of no more orgasms.

A secret she planned to keep.

But a secret she had also filed away to do something with later. Like once she'd had the baby and her stomach returned to some semblance of flat and she could rent one of those killer historical dresses and let Coop ravish her in it.

Yeah, something like that.

For now, she was sticking with brownies and gum and cheese-cake, and anything else she could discover.

Because she wanted him to feel as special as he made her feel.

Because he was different from her father, and their relationship was different from her parents'.

They each wanted to make the other person happy.

Coop grinned at her when he opened the bag and peeked inside, looping an arm around her neck and drawing her in and slanting his mouth over hers.

"Thanks, baby."

That alone made her heart grow.

And so, she wasn't going to stop finding ways to make Coop happy.

Just as she knew he was going to do the same for her.

———

"Let me get this straight," Coop's mom, Doreen, said in a clipped tone. "She's pregnant. It's not yours."

Yeah, her expression pretty much said it all.

Calle should have come prepared to this dinner, should have remembered that while she'd had a few months to get used to the idea of Coop being there for her and her baby, his parents hadn't.

She'd made him promise to tell his family the truth, not wanting a big secret, especially when the baby wasn't going to come out looking like Coop. It might not be the team or a random stranger's business to know that fact, but she'd figured their families should know the situation and be prepared for it.

But she hadn't really processed that the situation might not reflect well on her.

Of course, it wouldn't.

Shit.

She and Coop had spent a picture-perfect month together, and every day seemed better than the last. So, she hadn't really thought twice about meeting Coop's parents when he'd asked her. Yes, she knew they'd technically met, but it wasn't like this. She'd been a coach meeting her player's family, not a pregnant girl-friend attempting to survive the gauntlet of parental glaring.

Or, at least, Doreen was glaring.

She bit her lip, turned to glance at Coop's dad, Daniel. He stared back at her stonily. Double shit. He was glaring, too. "I'm—"

"It's mine," Coop said, cutting her off before she could tell his parents that he was under no financial or custodial obligation. That the baby was hers and hers alone, and while their relationship had been almost idyllic and she didn't want him to ever leave, she also wouldn't stop him from going.

"It's—" Doreen began again.

"The baby is mine," he said, tone not leaving room for negotiation. "I've been there for every appointment. I held back Calle's hair when she got sick, I've made the taco and Oreo shake runs at three A.M., I've watched the baby grow from the outside as her belly grows and from the inside as the pictures on the ultrasounds change." He slid his arm around her waist and hauled her against his side, keeping her there when she'd been trying to be respectful of his parents and keep a little space between them. Especially when the urge to jump his bones only seemed to increase the longer they were together.

Hormones?

Coop?

Still definitely Coop.

But his parents didn't get that. All they knew was a woman who potentially had power over him was pregnant from another man and might be trapping their son—

"I have sole parental rights," she blurted when it looked like Doreen was going to say something else. "Coop knows he has an out. He knows he just has to say the word, and he can leave."

She felt Coop's angry gaze on her face but kept talking.

"I wouldn't ever trap him or hurt his career. I love him." She cleared her throat. "He knows he can go—"

"Nothing is ever that simple, darlin'," Daniel said. "Coop's involved and an innocent will be involved. It's not so easy to just up and leave."

Coop's dad had spoken gently, so she knew he didn't mean it as a blow.

But it still felt like one anyway.

Her eyes filled with tears, stinging fuckers she tried to blink back and quickly failed at doing so. They dripped down her cheeks, dripping off her jaw. "I-I'm s-sorry," she sobbed. "Th-this is-isn't a ma-manipulation. I-I don't even kn-know why I'm crying—"

Embarrassed, she broke off, hands coming over her face.

But Coop pulled them away and turned her into his chest, holding her tight, then casually announced as she cried like a lunatic on his chest, "Calle's dad was a real asshole."

And then he kept talking, his voice gentle as gave a brief overview of her dad's asshole tendencies. Probably, she should have been upset that he was telling his parents, but she couldn't really be mad. It wasn't a state secret, and she was done being ashamed about it. Frankly, she was too much of a sobbing mess to gain control of herself enough to explain anyway.

After a few minutes, she managed to get control of herself and sniffed, wiping her face on his T-shirt before she pushed against his hold.

"What Coop said is the truth," she said, shifting to face his parents when he didn't let her go. "My dad wasn't a good person. But that also means I understand the stakes of him being involved. How important it is to all of us." She rested a hand on her belly. "Also, I'm sorry for the tears. I'm not normally like this, crying at the stupidest thing."

Doreen's face had softened slightly. "I cried when I was pregnant, too."

Calle grimaced. "Did it make you feel as ridiculous then as I do now?"

Daniel chuckled and Calle swiped her arm across her face. "I'm sorry—"

"Stop apologizing," Coop growled.

"I'm—" She broke off, steadied herself. "I fought against my attraction to Coop for two years, knowing that I would never do anything to put his job at risk. Then I fought him when my car broke down and he insisted on driving me to my first appointment. Then I fought him when he slowly wore me down with all the little things—holding back my hair when I lost my cookies, bringing me saltines and ginger ale afterward, and so many other thoughtful, small things that showed me he paid attention and he cared."

She turned and looked up at Coop, wanting him to know how much that meant. "I fought him until I knew he wasn't like my dad. I fought him until I couldn't fight him any longer."

He cupped her cheek, and he stared down at her, eyes intent. "And she still made me promise that I'd walk away without a second thought if it wasn't working." His gaze left hers, moved to his parents. "As though I hadn't already made my decision that I wasn't ever going to leave before I left that ginger ale in her office."

Silence.

Then Doreen smiled. "Just like your father."

Daniel stood and clapped Coop on the shoulder. "Can't fault you, son. She's like your mother. Too precious to give up."

And cue more tears.

This time however, Doreen shooed Coop away, ordering him and Daniel to pick up takeout, and then wrapped Calle in her arms and gave her the best Mom Hug ever.

"Shh, honey," she murmured into Calle's hair. "You never had a chance, did you?"

"No," Calle said. "I don't think I did. And thank you for being kind," she murmured. "I get why you wouldn't want Coop involved with me."

"My Coop is a good man." She pulled back, grasped Calle's shoulders lightly. "But he's also an Armstrong, which means he's stubborn as hell. He would have worn down a brick wall, let alone a red-blooded woman."

Calle smiled. "He was persistent."

"Because he's like my Daniel. Sees the treasure and holds on to it tightly."

Her brows drew down. "I'm not so sure I'm a treasure."

"That's why he's perfect for you, honey. He can see the treasure underneath all that protective wrapping." She tucked her arm around Calle. "And when you're ready, he'll help you show that treasure to the world instead of hiding it."

Calle sniffed. "No fair. You're going to make me cry again."

Doreen laughed. "Bring it on," she said. "I've got plenty of experience with tears."

And so, Calle rested her head on Doreen's shoulder, letting the tears come, letting go of the past and the pain, letting this woman into her heart, right alongside Coop. Because this was her future, and she wanted so much more for herself and her baby.

"He'll be there for you," Doreen murmured. "We all will be. No matter what. That's what it means to be an Armstrong."

She believed Doreen.

Unfortunately, sometimes believing in something wasn't enough.

SEVENTEEN

COOP

Several weeks had passed since Calle had met his parents and they'd flitted back down to San Diego, promising to return to the Bay Area for a visit before heading home.

The meeting hadn't started smooth, but it had ended with laughter and more hugs.

And with his mom calling to check in on Calle every couple of days.

And his dad calling to check to make sure he was taking care of Calle and that he followed through on the thing they'd discussed when they'd left his apartment to pick up takeout.

It was brilliant.

The perfect gift for Calle.

The single thing he could give her that would erase the lingering doubts in her head.

And it had come today.

He held the package as he strode down the hall, glad they were at the practice facility that day because it was closer to Calle's condo, and he couldn't wait to follow up the gift-giving by spending some quality time between her thighs.

Coop couldn't get enough of her pussy.

Thankfully, Calle couldn't seem to get enough of him licking her until she came, either.

He rounded the corner and approached her door, knocking once and then poking his head in carefully to make sure she wasn't in a meeting.

What he saw inside made his heart freeze in his chest.

Calle was there, obviously just finishing changing—and damn, but she sucked at fucking door locks. She was in a pair of faded jeans, the button held closed by a hair tie, her breasts encased in a sports bra, a T-shirt held out in front of her.

But that wasn't what made his heart seize.

No, his heart stopped working because of the blood.

So. Much. Blood.

Her eyes flew up to his, her arm reached out, face crumbling. "Coop," she said, and then her knees give out.

———

Later, he'd find out he'd shouted for help, rousing the offices next to him in seconds.

In that moment, all he was aware of was slamming through the door, too far away to catch Calle before she hit the floor, the blood staining the material between her legs.

Then Gabe was there, shoving him aside and issuing orders.

Coop held Calle's hand, willing her to open her eyes.

But she just lay there on the floor, unconscious.

A stretcher was brought in. She was packed off in it as he strode quickly alongside, never letting go of her hand.

In fact, Coop didn't let go until Gabe had to physically pry him away so they could wheel Calle back into the emergency department.

Leaving him alone in the waiting room.

And his woman fighting for the two lives that mattered most without him.

———

"Cooper?"

The voice came after many hours.

But about forty minutes before, a nurse had come out to tell him that Calle been stabilized and would be admitted upstairs to the maternity ward. That was it. No details on her or the baby's condition, just that she'd be admitted, and a doctor would speak with him soon. He'd switched waiting rooms at the same time, though he was no longer alone. A revolving door of Gold players had come and sat with him, not talking, thank God, but just sitting next to him, a silent support system.

They were the only thing keeping him from tearing his hair out.

Well, that and Mandy appearing, handing over a cup of coffee and then silently grabbing his free hand and wrapping it in both of hers.

She didn't tell him it would be okay.

She was just there.

And it was enough.

At least until he turned and saw it was Dr. Holdings calling his name. She looked grim. Fuck. She. Looked. Grim.

Mandy stood, released his hand, and nudged him in the direction.

"Go, Coop," she said.

Dr. Holdings held out an arm. "Come on back, now," she said. "Everything is okay."

He didn't relax. Not yet. "With both of them?"

A nod. "I know it was a scary situation, and Calle was lucky she was able to get here quickly. But things are stabilized now." She ran her badge over the lock and let him into the ward. "You know her placenta was low according to the last ultrasound?"

"The tech mentioned they would need to take another look."

"Unfortunately, it was lower than the technician realized. It's why she had so much bleeding, but she's feeling a lot better after the transfusion."

"Transfusion."

Dr. Holdings stopped and took his arm. "She's okay. The baby's okay."

Coop held his shit together.

"Likely, she'll need to deliver via C-section."

Okay, that wasn't the worst thing in the world.

"Also, she'll be on bed rest for the rest of the pregnancy."

"Fuck," he muttered.

"Yeah," Dr. Holdings said. "I figured that would be the more difficult part of this situation for her." She pointed to a door. "Calle's in there, probably sleeping, though she was trying to wait for you to come in so she could reassure you."

That made Coop's lips twitch and he shook his head in disbelief.

Reassure *him?*

She'd been bleeding so much that she'd needed a transfusion, and she was trying to stay awake to reassure *him?*

"Yeah, figured you'd have that reaction," the doctor said. "Go on in, and I'll be in later to check on her."

"Does she know?"

Dr. Holdings nodded. "Yes," she said. "I spoke with her just before I came out to get you."

Fucking hell.

Coop lifted his chin and pushed through the door, expecting to find a devastated woman in the bed. Instead, he found a chipper one.

That's right.

Chipper.

She smiled up at him. "Coop!"

He froze inside the door, unsure of what to do with this woman. He'd expected tears and sadness, instead he got . . . a wide smile and, "You look exhausted. Quick. Come here and let me tell you what happened so you can go home and rest up for the game."

The game?

Fuck the game.

He was somehow supposed to go home and sleep after seeing his Calle, his woman, the love of his fucking life collapse to the floor bleeding enough to need a transfusion, and then he was supposed to rest up for the game that night?

No fucking way.

"Coop."

He shook himself, crossed over to her, and sat in the chair at her bedside.

"I'm okay," she murmured, reaching for his hand.

Nope. None of this was okay.

"Baby, you're not okay," he snapped.

"The baby is okay. *I'm* okay." Her expression was gentled. "I know it was scary to see me like that. I mean, I was terrified before —" Here, she faltered for a second. "I was scared, and I got to spend part of it asleep."

Asleep.

A-fucking-sleep.

Coop shot to his feet and paced across the room, trying to find calm, trying to find rational when all he wanted to do was yank her in his arms and hold on to her forever.

But he couldn't do that right in this moment.

Because she was in a fucking hospital bed.

"Bed rest," he growled.

So calm and rational weren't within his grasp.

"What?" she asked.

"Doc said you were going on bed rest."

"I know, baby," she murmured. "It's fine. I've got a plan."

"You've got a plan?"

"I've already cleared it with Bernard, just in this exact case." A beat. "Not ideal, especially with playoffs starting in the next couple of weeks. Still, I'll be able to watch remotely and talk through an earpiece to Craig during games and practices. He'll relay the necessary information."

Craig was another assistant coach. Solid, but more comfortable with defense.

Which wasn't the point.

The point was his woman was in the hospital, just woken from unconsciousness after having had a blood transfusion, and she was talking about hockey. About plans. About fucking earpieces.

He dropped his chin to his chest.

Control. Control. Control—

"I'm okay," she repeated.

Fuck control.

His head jerked up. "You're not fucking okay," he snapped. "You scared the shit out of me and scared the shit out of the team. You have someone else's blood pumping through your body. You were unconscious for fucking hours. You—"

"I need you to not freak out."

He threw his hands up. "How can I possibly not freak out?" He stormed to her side, glaring down at her. "I was worried you were going to die. Fuck, baby. I was so damned worried and—"

His voice cracked.

Fuck.

He closed his eyes, sucked in long, slow breaths. "You didn't see the way you looked. How pale and still. I thought you were dead and even if you survived, I thought you'd lose the baby—"

A hand on his.

"I know, honey," she said. "I thought the same. I woke up and I thought she was gone—" A tear slid down her cheek. "But then Dr. Holdings came in and told me she was okay."

His breath froze in his lungs.

"I thought she was gone," she murmured. "And then I found out she wasn't. So, she's okay. I'm okay. *We're* okay." A beat. "It's over, and we've got to move on."

She'd fucking lost her mind, right along with all that blood.

"Did she tell you that?" Calle asked, squeezing his hand. "Coop?"

He blinked. "What?"

"Our little girl finally posed the right way for them to see she's a *she*, and Dr. Holdings didn't know that *I* didn't know," Calle said, eyes gentle. "So, she spilled the beans, and . . . we're going to have a little girl, Coop."

We're.

Our.

She continued talking while he absorbed that. Not the fact that the baby was a little girl, because he didn't give two shits about that.

Because Calle had said *we're* and *our.*

"And I don't know what I'm going to do with a little girl. I don't do pink or unicorns. I can't braid hair or do a messy bun. I can't even match clothes properly. I have to have the salespeople put them together in outfits and buy them that way." He moved, bending toward the bed as she kept talking. "I'm going to totally suck as the mom of a girl. I—*hey!*"

He'd shifted her gently to the side and crawled in next to her.

"You're okay," he murmured, cupping her cheek.

She nodded. "Yes, baby."

He carefully wound his arms around her and then tugged her against his chest, stroking a hand down her hair, down her back. "You're *really* okay."

"I'll allow this because you're terrified." She snuggled in. "But you need to leave in a little bit. To go home and sleep."

"I'm not going home," he muttered, the terror and anger faded, but his irritation still rampant.

In the fucking hospital and making plans for the offense.

The woman was insane.

"I love you."

The irritation faded. "I love you, too."

"You need to rest," she began.

He put a finger under her chin and tilted it up. "I'm *not* going."

She made a face. "I don't want you to upend your life just because—"

"My woman and our baby are in the hospital?" He snorted. "I can't see a better time to upend my life."

"Coop."

"Right," he muttered. "I thought we'd gotten past this, but I see that you've still got shit running through your brain."

"*Coop.*"

"No," he snapped. "I'm here. I'm not going to the fucking game, and you're fucking kidding yourself if you even think that Bernard or Stefan or fucking Craig would let me on the ice tonight. Hell, Brit would clobber me with her stick if I tried, even with your blessing." He made air quotes with one hand. "Further that, you know I'd be a liability because my mind would be right here." He kissed her forehead. "With you. In this bed. With you and our little girl."

Her lips parted, breath slipping out.

He pressed a kiss there. "And you know it," he murmured against her mouth. "You know I'd be a fucking mess, and it wouldn't be good for the team."

A tear slipped free, plunked onto his chest.

"You're scared, baby. You're scared because shit got real today, and you think I'm going to leave because of it." He tugged a strand of her disheveled hair. "Here's the thing. I'm not going anywhere."

More tears.

"I am scared," she whispered. "I thought I had it all together and was fine. I thought I knew that you were sticking around. But then I thought about me being on bed rest for the next four months and being a liability to the team. I'm going to be stuck at home, and you can live your life, and . . . I kept thinking that I need to make sure you live your life so that you won't leave me."

Fuck, she was killing him.

"Baby," he said gently. "What I don't think you get is that my life is shit without you."

"Coop!" she gasped on a half-laugh. "Don't say that. Before me, your life was—"

"A *half*-life."

She shook her head.

"The moment you decided to give me a chance was the moment I saw the world in full color. Fuck, baby, do you think I would have invested so much into someone who didn't?"

She bit her lip, tears stopping, but she didn't answer him.

"I'll tell you," he said. "The answer is no fucking way. I spent three hours searching for a store that could get me that giant ass jar of peanut butter, just because I wanted to see what your face looked like when I gave it to you." He rested his forehead against hers. "I snuck down to the hotel's kitchen to make sure the room service guy delivered my note along with the carrot cake. And"— he threaded his fingers through her hair, waited until her eyes met his—"when you told me you loved me, I was toast. The deal was done. I was yours. For-fucking-ever."

"You can't promise—"

He kissed her until they were both breathing hard.

"I can." Another press of his lips. "I will."

"Coop—"

His mouth slanted across hers, his tongue slipping inside, teasing hers out to play.

She pulled back. "You can't just keep kissing me to shut me up."

He leaned in. "I can try."

A sigh.

"I love you, sweetheart." Coop brushed his lips against hers. "And while I can promise you that I'm not leaving because I know it in the marrow of my bones, I know that's intangible. That's why I was bringing you these—"

He shifted, pulling the envelope out of the back pocket of his jeans. It was creased and folded to hell and back, but he'd somehow held on to it, not realizing until he'd been in the waiting room for some hours.

"What—?"

He put it in her hands. "Open it."

For once, she didn't argue and tore open the flap with shaking fingers, tugging the papers free, her eyes shooting up to his when she realized what those papers said.

"Adoption papers?"

Coop nodded.

"As soon as she's born, she's getting my name on the birth certificate and we're making it official." It was the thing he and his dad had talked about, and it made sense—he needed to protect both his girls.

He took the papers, carefully folded them back up. "She's mine. You're mine—"

She kissed *him* this time.

Cutting off his words.

Shutting *him* up for a change.

But Coop didn't mind, especially when she broke away and said, "I get it now." Before kissing him again and continuing to kiss him until Dr. Holdings interrupted them with a loud cough.

But before the doctor could speak, Calle tilted her face up so their gazes met and said, "Also, there is no way in fucking hell that you're playing tonight. Blue needs a line mate, not a hole on the ice." She nipped his jaw. "You're staying here with me." Then whispered in his ear, "Forever."

And Coop knew she meant it.

Because he whispered back, "Forever."

Epilogue

CALLE

Turned out she could coach via an earpiece, but it was so much better being on home ice when the Gold hoisted their second Cup win in franchise history.

It had been a hard-fought playoff run and an even harder final round.

But they'd won.

For the second time in three years.

And in many ways, it seemed like the end of an era.

Stefan had announced his plans to retire, and Mike seemed like he might follow him. Blane and Max only had one more year on each of their contracts. But Coop would be around.

He'd signed a five-year-multimillion-dollar deal, bolstered by the fact that he'd been on a tear when he'd returned the week after Calle had been discharged from the hospital.

There hadn't been any hesitation on his part. He'd simply terminated his lease while she was stuck in the hospital bed, moved his stuff into her place, and then had cleared and painted the second bedroom a bubblegum pink by the time she made it home.

He'd even bought a crib.

And changing table.

And if Calle hadn't already accepted that he was hers, furnishing the nursery so she didn't have to worry about it, would have cemented the fact. He'd left her with only the fun stuff, and she'd online-shopped her way to a unicorn-themed room.

Hell, it seemed the only thing to go with those bubblegum pink walls.

She smiled, watching from her seat on the bench, her toes barely grazing the ground, but following Dr. Holding's strict orders to a tee.

She'd been sprung from lockdown for Game Seven and had been ordered to keep her ass in a chair or on the bench whenever she wasn't actively coaching.

Which had been most of the night.

Because the Gold had destroyed the Rangers.

Absolutely obliterated them.

For her. She knew that it was for her and Coop and the little girl that Max wanted her to name Stanley—so not happening, by the way. But also, for themselves. Because they'd worked their asses off and were gelling at just the perfect time . . . and kismet happened for a second time.

Next season would probably be different.

The roster changes would make another journey here nearly impossible, even if repeating a championship run wasn't an almost insurmountable task.

But for the here and now, she and her giant, beached-whale-feeling body were going to enjoy the moment.

Brit and Stefan, side-by-side, their arms around each other as Kevin circled with the trophy, passing it off and then going right over to PR-Rebecca to steal her camera and kiss her soundly on the lips.

Blane holding his daughter in his arms, Mandy smiling from the hall.

Gabe and Nutritionist-Rebecca standing next to her and looking, rightfully, so damned proud.

Mike standing by the glass, staring at Sara, their bare hands pressed to the glass.

Angie and Brayden, Max's son, cheering like lunatics in the stands.

And Coop.

Coop skating toward her. She pushed up from the bench, her lips parting to offer her congratulations.

But he wasn't looking at *her*.

He was staring over her shoulder at . . . Bernard?

Um, what?

He walked right by her, stopping behind the bench and reaching for something that Bernard pulled out of his pocket.

Then he gently lifted her.

"What—?"

He butt landed her in a chair just inside the ice.

"What—?" She began again.

Coop didn't answer her, just pushed the chair a few feet away from the bench.

"Couldn't swing a recliner on the ice, baby."

"What—?"

Her third what-beginning question was cut off when Coop went down on one knee.

In full view of the cameras, in full view of the team, in full view of the twenty-thousand fans.

She knew the moment the crowd realized what was happening.

The cheers became deafening.

She couldn't focus on them, or that fact that her ears were ringing.

Because Coop was on his knee with a ring box open on his palm, and his mouth was forming words she couldn't hear but could discern on his lips even without the on-one-knee-open-box-with-a-glittering-ring situation happening.

"Will you marry me?"

"Yes!" she shouted, knowing he wouldn't be able to hear her, but also knowing that he'd get it anyway.

And he did.

Because his smile went wide, and the chair almost tipped over when he lurched up to kiss her.

And the photograph PR Rebecca caught of the two of them in each other's arms, laughing and kissing with Coop's hands on the outside of its frame as he stopped the chair from falling over was her favorite picture ever.

She had it blown up and framed.

It hung on the wall in the living room of their new house.

Right next to the first picture of Coop holding Emma "Stanley" Armstrong in his arms—taken seconds after she'd been born and milliseconds after she'd stolen both of their hearts.

It wasn't going anywhere either.

———

LIAM

He was fucking up.

As usual.

He'd had a particularly bad practice, after a particularly bad game, after a particularly bad *series* of games, and he knew that his hopes of staying with the San Francisco Gold were quickly becoming slim-to-none.

The name Williamson used to strike fear in the league.

His grandfather, his father, his two older brothers had been forces to be reckoned with.

He . . . was scraping by.

Four teams in four seasons.

Shitty stats.

And somehow, he'd gotten picked up off waivers by the Gold,

reigning league champions, who were in the midst of a rebuilding season after losing some of their big stars.

He was expected to fill a hole.

But how in the fuck was *he*, the smallest and least scary of the Williamsons supposed to fill a hole when he'd barely earned a roster spot?

Fuck.

He put his head down, tugged the collar of his jacket up.

He should just call it already, put the league behind him and find a new career. Math had been his strong suit—maybe he should go back and be an accountant. He could run his brothers' multimillion-dollar fortunes, help them eek out a few more dollars and—

"Watch out!"

The warning came a second too late.

He'd already stepped off the curb, already put himself into the range of the car that was blowing through the red light, tearing through the intersection, not giving a shit that there were pedestrians walking—

Well, of all the ways to go, at least this would be quick.

But just as the car came within an inch of him, Liam found himself jerked back onto the curb, his one-hundred-and-eighty-pound frame becoming unwieldy and clumsy.

Kind of like on the ice over the last few years.

That was the last thought before he found himself sprawled, ass first onto the San Franciscan sidewalk.

Gross.

"What the fuck?" a female voice snapped.

The same female voice that had warned him.

"Do you have a fucking death wish?" she yelled, foot tapping, arms crossed, and seeming way too small to have been able to have hauled his ass back onto the curb.

Liam thought that he just might, if it meant that he got to be rescued by a woman who looked like this one. He opened his mouth to reply.

But apparently didn't work fast enough.

Because the woman, the beautiful, curvy female made a disgusted noise and strode away from him.

He watched her go, watched that gorgeous ass stride down the sidewalk and stop outside a storefront. By the time he pushed to his feet, she'd pulled out her keys and unlocked the door, disappearing inside.

Liam glanced at the sign overhead.

Golden Gate Martial Arts.

He thought of the swaying hips as she'd stomped away. He thought of the fiery words she'd snapped at him. He thought of the pretty brown eyes and lush lips incongruously paired with enough strength to pull him back.

And suddenly, he thought that, hockey or not, he might just want to stay in San Francisco after all.

––––––

Thank you for reading! I hope you loved meeting Calle and Coop as much as I loved writing them! The next book in the Gold Hockey series is CENTERED.

He was about to be traded...and the woman he loved would be left behind.

CLICK HERE TO READ CENTERED>

And if you enjoyed COASTING, you'll love the sexy, sweet, and close-knit Breakers Hockey crew. The first book in the series, BROKEN, is now live!

> *"It is sexy, hot, adorable and such a fun read. You will not be able to put this down!"* —Amazon Reviewer

I'd brought him home thinking that for once in my life I

would live a little. Now weeks later...I was puking my guts up and had a pink stick with a plus sign on it declaring my future.

DOWNLOAD BAD NIGHT STAND FOR FREE HERE

>

I so appreciate your help in spreading the word about my books, including sharing with friends! Please leave a review on your favorite book site!

You can also join my Facebook group, the Fabinators, for exclusive giveaways and sneak peeks of future books.

SIGN UP FOR ELISE FABER'S NEWSLETTER HERE:
https://www.elisefaber.com/newsletter

———

Want a free bonus story? Hate missing Elise's new releases? Love contests, exclusive excerpts and giveaways?
Then signup for Elise's newsletter here!
https://www.elisefaber.com/newsletter

———

And join Elise's fan group, the Fabinators https://www.facebook.com/groups/fabinators for insider information, sneak peaks at new releases, and fun freebies! Hope to see you there!

Gold Hockey Series

GOLD HOCKEY

Did you miss any of the Gold Hockey books?
Find information about the full series here.
Or keep reading for a sneak peek into each of the books below!

Blocked
Gold Hockey Book #1
Get your copy at https://www.elisefaber.com/blocked

BRIT

The first question Brit always got when people found out she played ice hockey was *"Do you have all of your teeth?"*

The second was *"Do you, you know, look at the guys in the locker room?"*

The first she could deal with easily—flash a smile of her full set of chompers, no gaps in sight. The second was more problematic. Especially since it was typically accompanied by a smug smile or a coy wink.

Of course she looked. *Everybody* looked once. Everyone snuck a glance, made a judgment that was quickly filed away and shoved deep down into the recesses of their mind.

And she meant *way* down.

Because, dammit, she was there to play hockey, not assess her teammates' six packs. If she wanted to get her man candy fix, she could just go on social media. There were shirtless guys for days filling her feed.

But that wasn't the answer the media wanted.

Who cared about locker room dynamics? Who gave a damn whether or not she, as a typical heterosexual woman, found her fellow players attractive?

Yet for some inane reason, it *did* matter to people.

Brit wasn't stupid. The press wanted a story. A scandal. They were desperate for her to fall for one of her teammates—or better yet the captain from their rival team—and have an affair that was worthy of a romantic comedy.

She'd just gotten very good at keeping her love life—as nonexistent as it was—to herself, gotten very good at not reacting in any perceptible way to the insinuations.

So when the reporter asked her the same set of questions for the thousandth time in her twenty-six years, she grinned— showing off those teeth—and commented with a sweetly innocent "Could've sworn you were going to ask me about the coed showers." She waited for the room-at-large to laugh then said, "Next question, please."

–Get your copy at https://www.elisefaber.com/blocked

Backhand
Gold Hockey Book #2
Get your copy at https://www.elisefaber.com/backhand

SARA

"Sorry I messed up your sketch," he rumbled.

She nibbled on the side of her mouth, biting back a smile. "Sorry I stole your hand for so long."

He shrugged. "My mom's an artist. I get it."

Well, there went her battle with the smile. Her lips twitched and her teeth came out of hiding. If there was one thing that Sara had, it was her smile. It had been her trademark in her competition days.

Which were long over.

Her mouth flattened out, the grin slipping away. Time to go, time to forget, to move on, to rebuild. "Thanks," she said and extended a hand.

Then winced and dropped it when her ribs cried out in protest.

"You okay?" he asked, head tilting, eyes studying her.

"Fine." And out popped her new smile. The fake one. Careful of her aching side, she shrugged into her backpack. "I've got to go." She turned, ponytail flapping through the hair to land on her opposite shoulder.

"That—" He touched her arm. "Wait. I *know* I know you."

She froze. That was the second time he'd said that, and now they were getting into dangerous territory. Recognition meant . . . no. She couldn't.

There had been a time when *everyone* had known her. Her face on Wheaties boxes, her smile promoting toothpaste and credit cards alike.

That wasn't her life any longer.

"Thanks again. Bye." She started to hurry away.

"Wait." A hand dropped on to her shoulder, thwarting her escape, and she hissed in pain.

"Sorry," he said, but he didn't release her. Instead, he shifted his grip from her aching shoulder down to her elbow and when she didn't protest, he exerted gentle pressure until Sara was facing him again. "It's just that know I *know* you."

No. This wasn't happening.

"You're Sara Jetty."

Her body went tense.

Oh God. This was *so* happening.

"It's me." He touched his chest like she didn't know he was talking about himself, and even as she was finally recognizing the color of his eyes, the familiar curve of his lips and line of his jaw, he said the worst thing ever, "Mike Stewart."

Oh *shit*.

—Get your copy at https://www.elisefaber.com/backhand

Boarding
Gold Hockey Book #3
Get your copy at https://www.elisefaber.com/boarding

MANDY

Hockey players had the *best* asses.

No pancake bottoms, these men—and *women*—could fill out a pair of jeans. She wanted to squeeze it, to nibble it, bounce a dime—

Mandy dropped her chin to her chest, losing sight of the Sorting Hat cupcakes she'd been pondering.

Blane with his yummy ass had a unique way of distracting her.

No, it wasn't even distraction, per se. He had *always* been able to get under her skin.

And that was very, very bad for her.

"Ugh," she said, tossing her phone onto her desk and standing, knowing that she wouldn't be able to sit still now.

Nope, she needed about forty laps in the pool and a good hard fu—

Run, her mind blurted, almost yelling at the mental voice of her inner devil. *A good hard run.*

Unfortunately, the cajoling tone wasn't completely drowned out. *Some sexy horizontal time with Blane would be more fun—*

But the rest of the enticing words were lost as the roar of the crowd suddenly penetrated through the layers of concrete. Her stomach twisted. Mandy could tell, even before her eyes made it to the television, that it wasn't in celebration of a goal or a good hit either.

This was fury, a collective of outrage.

She was on her feet the moment she saw the prone form lying so still face down on the ice.

Her gut twisted when she spotted the curving line of a numeral two on the back of the player's jersey.

"Not him," she said and the words were familiar, a sentiment she had whispered, had *prayed* a thousand times before. She needed the camera angle to shift, for her to be able to see more clearly *who* was hurt. "Not him."

Then Dr. Carter was on the ice and the player moved slightly, rolling away from the camera, giving a full shot of his back and the matching twos adorning his jersey.

Fuck. Not him. Not Blane.

And that was when she saw the pool of blood.

—Get your copy at https://www.elisefaber.com/boarding

Benched
Gold Hockey Book #4
Get your copy at https://www.elisefaber.com/benched

MAX

He started up the car, listening and chiming in at the right places as Brayden talked all things video game.

But his mind was unfortunately stuck on the fact that women were not to be trusted.

He snorted. Brit—the Gold's goalie and the first female in the NHL—and Mandy—the team's head trainer—would smack him around for that sentiment, so he silently amended it to: *most* women were not to be trusted.

There. Better, see?

Somehow, he didn't think they'd see.

He parked in the school's lot, walked Brayden in, and received the appropriate amount of scorn from the secretary for being thirty minutes late to school, then bent to hug Brayden.

"I'll pick you up today," he said.

Brayden smiled and hugged him tightly. Then he whispered something in his ear that hit Max harder than a two-by-four to the temple.

"If you got me a new mom, we wouldn't be late for school."

"Wh-what?" Max stammered.

"Please, Dad? Can you?"

And with that mind fuck of an ask, Brayden gave him one more squeeze and pushed through the door to the playground, calling, "Love you!" over his shoulder.

Then he was gone, and Max was standing in the office of his son's school struggling to comprehend if he had actually just heard what he'd heard.

A new mom?

Fuck his life.

—Get your copy at https://www.elisefaber.com/benched

Breakaway
Gold Hockey Book #5
Get your copy at https://www.elisefaber.com/breakaway

BLUE

"Thanks for the ride."

"Try not to go out and get a fresh bimbo to ride tonight. I hear STIs on are the rise in the city."

Blue sighed, turned back to face her. "Really?"

She shrugged, smirk teasing the edges of her mouth, drawing his focus to the lushness of her lips. "Just watching out for Max's teammate."

He rolled his eyes. "Not hardly."

"Okay, how about I'm trying to prevent you from spreading STIs to the female populace."

"I'm clean, and I'm smart," he told her. "Condoms all the way."

"Ew."

Except there was something about the way she said it that made Blue stiffen and take notice. Because . . . he stared into her eyes, watched as the pale blue darkened to royal, saw her lips part, and her suck in a breath.

Holy shit.

"You're attracted to me."

Her jaw dropped. "No fucking way," she said, too quickly, pink dancing on the edges of her cheekbones. "You're delusional."

Blue got close.

Real close.

Anna licked her lips.

And fuck it all, he kissed that luscious mouth.

—Breakaway, https://www.elisefaber.com/breakaway

Breakout
Gold Hockey Book #6
Get your copy at https://www.elisefaber.com/breakout

PR-REBECCA

A fucking perfect hockey fairy tale.

Shaking her head, because she knew firsthand that fairy tales didn't exist outside of rom-coms and occasionally between alpha sports heroes and their chosen mates, Rebecca slipped through the corridor and stepped onto the Gold's bench.

Lots of dudes in suits—of both the boardroom *and* the hockey variety—were hugging.

On the ice. Near the goals. On the bench.

It was a proverbial hug-fest.

And she was the cynical bitch who couldn't enjoy the fact

that the team she was with had just won the biggest hockey prize of them all.

"I knew you'd be like this."

Rebecca turned her focus from Brit, who was skating with the huge silver cup, to the man—no, to the *boy* because no matter how pretty and yummy he was, Kevin was still a decade younger than her—leaning oh so casually against the boards.

"Nice goal," she told him.

A shrug. "Blue made a nice pass."

And dammit, the fact that he wasn't an arrogant son of a bitch made her like him more.

She nodded at the cup. "You should go have your turn."

"I'll get mine," he said with another shrug.

She frowned, honestly confused. "You don't want—"

Suddenly he was in front of her on the bench, towering over her even though she was wearing her four-inch power heels. "You know what I want?"

Rebecca couldn't speak. Her breath had whooshed out of her in the presence of all that sweaty, hockey god-ness. Fuck he was pretty and gorgeous and . . . so fucking masculine that her thighs actually clenched together.

She wanted to climb him like a stripper pole.

"Do you?" he asked again when her words wouldn't come. "Want to know what I want?"

She nodded.

He bent, lips to her ear. "You, babe," he whispered. "I. Want. You."

Then he straightened and jumped back onto the ice, leaving her gaping after him like she had less than two brain cells in her skull.

The worst part?

She wanted him, too.

Had wanted him since the moment she'd laid eyes on the sexy as sin hockey god.

"Trouble," she murmured. "I'm in *so* much fucking trouble."

—Breakout, https://www.elisefaber.com/breakout

Checked
Gold Hockey Book #7
Get your copy at https://www.elisefaber.com/checked

"Rebecca."

She kept walking.

She might work with Gabe, but she sure as heck wasn't on speaking terms with him. He'd dismissed her work, ignored her contribution to the team. He'd made her feel small and unimportant and—

She kept walking.

"*Rebecca.*"

Not happening. Her car was in sight, thank fuck. She beeped the locks, reached for the handle.

He caught her arm.

"Baby—"

"I am *not* your baby, and you don't get to touch me." She ripped herself free, started muttering as she reached for the handle of her car again. "You don't even like me."

He stepped close, real close. Not touching her, not pushing the boundary she'd set, and yet he still got really freaking close. Her breath caught, her chin lifted, her pulse picked up. "That. Is. Where. You're. Wrong."

She froze.

"What?"

His mouth dropped to her ear, still not touching, but near enough that she could feel his hot breath.

"I like you, Rebecca. Too fucking much."

Then he turned and strode away.

—Checked, https://www.elisefaber.com/checked

ALSO BY ELISE FABER

Billionaire's Club (all stand alone)
Bad Night Stand

Bad Breakup

Bad Husband

Bad Hookup

Bad Divorce

Bad Fiancé

Bad Boyfriend

Bad Blind Date

Bad Wedding

Bad Engagement

Bad Bridesmaid

Bad Swipe

Bad Girlfriend

Bad Best Friend

Bad Billionaire's Quickies

Gold Hockey (all stand alone)
Blocked

Backhand

Boarding

Benched

Breakaway

Breakout

Checked

Coasting

Centered

Charging

Caged

Crashed

A Gold Christmas

Cycled

Caught

Cap

Breakers Hockey (all stand alone)

<u>Broken</u>

<u>Boldly</u>

<u>Breathless</u>

<u>Ballsy</u>

<u>Bewitched</u>

Love, Action, Camera (all stand alone)

Dotted Line

Action Shot

Close-Up

End Scene

Meet Cute

***Love After Midnight* (all stand alone)**

Rum And Notes

Virgin Daiquiri

On The Rocks

Sex On The Seats

Life Sucks Series (all stand alone)
Train Wreck

Hot Mess

Dumpster Fire

Clusterf*@k

FUBAR (March 29,2022)

Roosevelt Ranch Series (all stand alone, series complete)
Disaster at Roosevelt Ranch

Heartbreak at Roosevelt Ranch

Collision at Roosevelt Ranch

Regret at Roosevelt Ranch

Desire at Roosevelt Ranch

Phoenix Series (read in order)
Phoenix Rising

Dark Phoenix

Phoenix Freed

Phoenix: LexTal Chronicles (rereleasing soon, stand alone, Phoenix world)
From Ashes

In Flames

To Smoke

KTS Series
Riding The Edge

Crossing The Line

Leveling The Field

Scorching The Earth

Cocky Heroes World

Tattooed Troublemaker

ABOUT THE AUTHOR

USA Today bestselling author, Elise Faber, loves chocolate, Star Wars, Harry Potter, and hockey (the order depending on the day and how well her team -- the Sharks! -- are playing). She and her husband also play as much hockey as they can squeeze into their schedules, so much so that their typical date night is spent on the ice. Elise changes her hair color more often than some people change their socks, loves sparkly things, and is the mom to two exuberant boys. She lives in Northern California. Connect with her in her Facebook group, the Fabinators or find more information about her books at www.elisefaber.com.

f facebook.com/elisefaberauthor

a amazon.com/author/elisefaber

BB bookbub.com/profile/elise-faber

O instagram.com/elisefaber

g goodreads.com/elisefaber

P pinterest.com/elisefaberwrite